Jerry's Ghosts

The Mystery of the Blind Tower

Other books by Sarah Sargent

Jonas McFee, A.T.P.
Seeds of Change

Jerry's Ghosts

The Mystery of the Blind Tower

By SARAH SARGENT

Bradbury Press/New York

Maxwell Macmillan Canada/Toronto
Maxwell Macmillan International
New York/Oxford/Singapore/Sydney

Bradbury Press
Macmillan Publishing Company
866 Third Avenue
New York, NY 10022

Maxwell Macmillan Canada, Inc.
1200 Eglinton Avenue East
Suite 200
Don Mills, Ontario M3C 3N1

Macmillan Publishing Company is part of the Maxwell Communication
Group of Companies.

First edition
Printed and bound in the United States of America
10 9 8 7 6 5 4 3 2 1

Library of Congress Cataloging-in-Publication Data
Sargent, Sarah, date.
Jerry's ghosts : the mystery of the blind tower / by Sarah
Sargent.—1st ed.
        p.   cm.
Summary: Sixth grader Jerry discovers two ghostly children,
trapped with their mad scientist uncle in the nineteenth-century
mansion that was their former home, and sets them free.
ISBN 0-02-778035-X
[1. Ghosts—Fiction.]   I. Title.
PZ7.S2479Je   1992
[Fic]--dc20   91-21971

For Dora Jane and Cutting Johnson

Jerry's Ghosts

The Mystery of the Blind Tower

". . . People have heard something like a train whistle coming from inside at night."

I

Someday the world would know about Jerry Roberts. He wasn't sure if he'd be famous as a performer or an inventor or from doing something brave that got in all the papers and on national TV. Jerry pictured it all those ways. But the last case was the one he came back to most often in his daydreams. . . .

A building is on fire. He darts inside, slipping past the lines of spectators, ignoring the gasps. "That boy can't go in there!" "Stop that boy!"

Crouching close to the floor, Jerry snakes his way to the back bedroom where the baby is choking, ready to breathe its last. Blackened beams are falling right and left; then, finally, as he emerges holding the baby, the roof caves in with a tremendous roar. Jerry stands for a moment, dazed by the cheers of the crowd. He hands the baby to its mother, a

1

beautiful young widow who kisses him.

Or, he's in the store down the corner from his place in New York City. He's a producer, wearing a red tie with tiny lions on it and shiny hundred-dollar shoes, just picking up a box of cereal or something. That's when a hood pulls a gun and nearly scares the sweet old white-haired man behind the counter to death.

What does Jerry do? He grabs the greaseball around the neck from behind and wrestles him to the floor, expertly flipping the gun out of his hand to the counter where the white-haired man picks it up. They tie up the punk and call the police. A small crowd gathers and cheers wildly as Jerry modestly attempts to slip away with his box of cereal.

"Gee, Mr. Roberts, I'd never have dreamed a big producer like you could pull something like that. Anytime you want anything in my store, it's yours for free," the old man tells him.

Jerry poured a second bowl of Miracle Puffs and rubbed a piece of paper towel into the milk he'd spilled. He sighed. Sure, Jerry, sure, he muttered to himself. Last time he'd taken a look at himself in the mirror, what had come to mind? You know those rubber squeak toys they give to babies? The pink ones with big ears and round tummies? Add a pair of glasses and you've got Jerry.

Okay, so what? He had to keep his perspective, right? Lots of sixth grade boys were kind of short. Boys grow later than girls. And most famous people will tell you they weren't exactly popular in elementary school. He knew that from reading his mom's *People* magazine. She bought it every week at the grocery store.

Jerry's dad drove a truck and was on the road most of the time. Besides, he'd married somebody else and had three other kids in Arkansas. Jerry hardly ever saw him. Once in a while he'd call. But that would end up with him calling Jerry "sport" and Jerry not able to think of anything to say.

His mom was a singer. At least, she *thought* she was a singer. She'd actually worked a day job, at Kmart in the housewares, up until a couple of weeks ago when she'd lost her mind.

"I've got a chance to make it, Jer," she'd said, sitting at the kitchen table, balancing her bare foot against the edge of the tabletop, painting her toenails lavender. "You wouldn't want me to miss this chance. Anyway, what's the big deal? One school's pretty much like the next one. Am I right? And that buddy of yours, Claxton, is nothing to write home about. Mom'll keep you while I'm on the road with the boys. Three months and I'll be back, we'll figure out what to do. We'll be a team again, am I right?"

She smiled at him, a warm smile through her drifting straight tan hair, but she wasn't looking at Jerry. Her eyes were distant, focused on the crowds that would be clapping and yelling and stomping when she sang.

She couldn't even get Clayton's name right. "I don't like it there. I like the city. I don't want to live with Grandma." Jerry knew if he whined he'd be lost. He hated himself for asking since he knew what the answer would be. He bit his lip, but the inevitable question came, by itself. "Why couldn't I go with you?"

"The road is no place for a child." His mom screwed the top back on the nail polish with a twist. She tossed her long hair over her shoulder in a quick gesture. She didn't look at him. He knew she felt guilty. "You'll be fine at Mom's. The air's clean. It's a Beaver Cleaver town."

So, two weeks later, Jerry was sitting at the kitchen table, suitcase packed, having his last breakfast before she drove him to the bus for East Bent, Grandma's boring little town in Wisconsin where people stooped down and cut their grass with the scissors so it'd line up with the sidewalk. Seriously, he'd seen the old guy next door to Grandma actually do that. And the same guy dug trenches beside his walk to keep any weed from touching the cement.

Jerry's bike tires had slipped into the hole and he'd nearly killed himself.

Jerry and his mom took out the garbage and all, but they didn't waste time making their place so neat it was a death trap. Jerry was a reader, a thinker, even a little bit of a dreamer. He liked piles of this and that around. He always had six or eight library books in a stack on his floor. And the newest Marvel comics plus a couple of older issues that he might want to check out again. And he usually left his clothes dumped at the end of the bed until his mom sent him to the Laundromat. Why put away stuff that you'll just take out again?

Jerry had good reason for wanting to stay in the city. He had been planning probably to be a writer or a producer ever since he'd gotten to know Clayton's Uncle Bob, who wrote for a magazine. Writers have to be where it's happening. Not stuck off in some little town where people thought it was a big deal if a sunflower grew extra tall. Seriously. Last time he and Mom had visited Grandma, there'd been a big color picture on the front page of the paper showing an old guy with his ten-foot-tall sunflower looming up behind him like a giant floor lamp.

"You all set, kid?" His mom came out of her room, jingling the car keys. Jerry sighed and dumped his bowl in the sink, and they were on their way.

II

THINK YOUR GRATE, CITY KID? YOU DIE. That note was on Jerry's desk the second morning at school in East Bent. There was a huge kid across from him who smelled like sour milk and had a neck like a walrus. He probably shaved. Twice he'd stuck out his foot to trip Jerry when he went to sharpen his pencil.

No matter what his mom said, Jerry was not sure he'd survive three months. He was scuffing along the sidewalk on a Tuesday evening, bringing Grandma back a carton of milk from the store. The air had a haze to it. Clayton's Uncle Bob had told them, "A writer can't just *look*. Seeing won't hack it. A writer's got to *smell* and *listen* for a story. *Taste* it, even." And truly, in October in Wisconsin, you could almost taste the dark coming by five

6

o'clock. A sort of heavy smoky taste, Jerry thought, like he'd eaten sausage. Spring nights tasted different. Like banana ice cream.

He turned a corner and started down the creepier part of the walk. Huge old houses from way back, with roofs like witches' hats and shadowy porches. The worst of all was the public museum, where they were about to go on a class trip. Starting past it, Jerry decided it was the scariest building he'd ever seen. A tower bulged off one end and dormer windows lined the upper story like droopy-lidded lizard eyes. Passing the spiky iron fence, with the October fog floating in with the dusk, Jerry would have been scared if he hadn't been too sensible to believe stories about vampires and voodoo and zombies.

Being dead wasn't sleeping or floating around on a cloud in the sky somewhere. It was just going out, like a light. Jerry was proud that he'd never been spooked by Halloween ghosts and vampires.

He scuffed through the yellow leaves that spattered the sidewalk. The front windows of the museum glinted at him, reflecting the sinking sun. Jerry dribbled his free hand, the one that wasn't holding the milk, against the iron spikes as he walked by, feeling them flick past like telephone poles from a train window.

Two children were standing in the shadows of

the front entrance, a girl a little taller than Jerry and a boy who looked four or five. The boy wore a white shirt, like for church, and dark pants. The girl's dress came almost to her ankles and she had fat curls down to her shoulders that swayed when she leaned forward toward the little boy. Jerry caught his breath. They seemed to have a ghostly light around them. For a second, he was almost terrified. Then he told himself he was acting like an East Bent hick. Most likely they'd been in a pageant at the museum, he told himself; a play about the old days or something.

The gate was chained. A big padlock dangled around the post. "Did you get locked in?" Jerry stopped at the gate and called down to the girl and boy. It would be hard to climb that spiky fence. Impossible in the long dress the girl was wearing. "Is there another gate?"

The girl wheeled toward him, her face a white oval against the dark shadows of the overhanging porch roof. Even at the end of the winding walk, fifty feet away, Jerry saw her stiffen. Her eyes were wide, her mouth half open. She stared at him as if he were a ghost. Jerry had never seen such terror on any human face.

"You want to get out?" he called to them again. She shook her head then, the curls swinging across her face. She held up her hand, palm out, and pushed away, signaling him to leave.

"No," her voice floated down to him, distant like a radio somebody had left on upstairs. "Go away."

"Okay, okay," he called back, stung that the girl was so nasty when he was just trying to help, bewildered that anyone could be so frightened of him. The girl held on to the little boy's hand and hitched up her skirt with her other hand. Leading him, she scurried back into the bushes beside the front entrance. Jerry stared. The bushes were thick evergreens full of prickly needles. How did she move through them as easily as she did? He watched the white blur of her dress and the boy's shirt as they passed behind the screen of dark branches. And, as he watched, he saw that something was even stranger. The bushes didn't quiver. How could two people tromp through a hedge without shaking a single limb?

They floated through the bushes to the north end of the building, beside the gray stone tower with the creaking weather vane on top. Then they vanished. It was not possible. Jerry knew that. But one second they were there. The next they weren't. He ran along the fence and peered behind the tower as best he could. Nobody.

"Whaah?" Jerry frowned. The shadows under the porch had deepened. The museum windows flashed like mirror sunglasses. Fear sending icy spears down his back, Jerry turned and ran.

III

Mattie knew they shouldn't have been out. Not before dark. It was little Edward's fault. He begged and begged and it was like water dripping on a stone and finally she couldn't say no one more time. The museum was locked; the people had gone home. Why did that boy have to be walking past the minute they formed themselves outside the wall?

Sickening normal boy, wrapped in skin, hurrying home to his dinner. She'd started like a deer at the sight of him outside the gate, waving and calling to them.

"Is that a real boy? Mattie, let's go see. Please." Little Edward had caught her hand, pulling her forward.

Mattie had held him back with one hand and gestured the boy away with the other. He'd thought they were locked in. "No," she'd called. "Go away."

"Yes," Edward had insisted. "I want to see the real boy."

"Hush. You know better than that." Mattie had pulled him sideways, into the bushes, dissolving through them until they were beside the tower. Then they faded back through the stone. Mattie could see and hear, but her body could not taste or smell or touch. Even so, she was sure she smelled a mustiness, felt a chill as they passed through the stone.

"Real boys are disagreeable, Edward," she said in a prissy voice, trying to remember how Mama had sounded. "They fight. They are loud and tiresome. You're better off here with me."

"I hate you, Mattie. You are mean. I want to see the real boy!" Edward pulled free and hunched down beside the wall in the dim tower room. He was trying to make her think he'd go outside without her, and someday he would.

Uncle did not want anyone to see them. Mattie knew they had to obey Uncle. She always called Uncle *him* to Edward in a scary voice so her little brother would know how important it was to mind. But for how long will a four-year-old pay attention? And Edward had already been four so terribly terribly long. It was getting harder and harder to make him listen.

"Real boys are no fun," she told him. "They have to use doors, the way we did before, you remember. They bump into things. They can't play train and tunnel the way we do." That was Edward's favorite game. At night, once the museum closed, they went through the wall. Edward loved to race through the familiar rooms, round and round, under the stairs, choo-chooing at the top of his lungs. The train had been his favorite thing. Papa had taken him to watch when it stopped at the station.

"I can't remember. Mattie, I can't remember 'Before.' You tell me."

Really he did. She knew that from the way he darted away from her at night in the museum, going to the upstairs alcove where the museum people had left some of their things on display. It had been their house before it was a museum. In that sweet short other life, they had lived there with Papa and Mama.

"This time of day, Edward, in the Before Time, was when Mama lit the gaslights. You remember? And Cook was getting dinner? And we smelled it— soup simmering, chicken roasting. You remember chicken, Edward?" Mattie paused, letting the memories flood in. The delicious tender meat, dripping with juice, the tender, fluffy stuffing, the blackberry jelly, the puddings and whipped cream and candied cherries. The smell of rain on the stones at the front door . . . the rose smell of Mama's toilet water when she kissed them good-night.

"Maybe I do, Mattie," Edward said in a suddenly still voice. "Maybe I remember chicken."

Mattie closed her eyes. The memories washed over her, warming even the dry husk that was left of her, the shimmery film that was her nothingbody.

IV

A block away, Jerry stopped running. He leaned against a telephone pole and reasoned with himself. The sun had been reflecting off the windows. Maybe that had dazzled his sight. The bushes were lumpy and could have looked like people standing there. Of course, he'd *heard* the girl call out to him. But Uncle Bob had told Clayton and him how your senses could fool you.

"That's what accounts for abominable snowmen and flying saucers, you boys believe me. A twig snaps out in the middle of nowhere and some joker sees a big hairy monster clear as I'm seeing you. He's not lying, either. Down to the thumbs fat as Ping-Pong paddles. You know when you watch TV all you *really* see is a bunch of dots? Your brain makes the picture. Well, everybody has a little movie

15

projector running inside his head, ready to put on just about any spook show you can dream up. All you need is one little detail your brain reads wrong, and it's ready with the whole feature film. Living color and sound to boot. I've seen it over and over. Little old ladies, sure, but even sheriffs and air-traffic controllers and whatnot. You take a sheriff in North Dakota, driving down one of those empty roads in the dark, he's liable to see *anything*."

Jerry shifted the milk carton to his other hand. Not liking the clamminess of it, he cradled it in the crook of his arm. His palms were cold and sweaty enough. He'd seen the children pass through the bushes like they were made of air. He'd seen them disappear through the wall of the stone tower. Was somebody making a fool of him? Was he making one of himself?

This was Tuesday. Thursday was the class trip. To the museum. He'd been thinking it would be boring. Now, though the hair on the back of his neck prickled, he was looking forward to it. Now, while the class was trooping through looking at the exhibits, he'd have a chance to watch for clues. He'd be on his guard. Maybe it was possible to trick him once, Jerry admitted. But not twice. Whatever was going on, he'd get to the bottom of it.

"No running. No pushing." Mrs. Craig herded

16

them off the bus in the museum parking lot on Thursday afternoon. Usually the class listened to her, but nobody paid much attention on a class-trip day. The class tumbled noisily up the walk and toward the front door. Jerry glanced nervously over his shoulder into the evergreen bushes as he bobbed along with the crowd. The doorway was wide and covered, a place for people to drive up to in their carriages in the old days.

The steps were stone, the doors massive oak with a pull ring to open them. The kid with the walrus neck got there first, of course, and yanked the ring so that it resounded against the wood. *Booong.* Jerry scurried inside, the sound echoing in his head. The wide main hall was lit by a big stained-glass window on the stair landing opposite the door. The banisters were carved dark wood and the window was pink, white, and purple with some gold. It was a picture of two women picking sheaves of wheat in a field in front of a mountain range. Jerry stood looking up at it.

"You like to live in a place like this?" Crystal, the girl who sat across from him, was beside his elbow.

"I might," he said, being cool. Crystal had long blond hair and a turned-up nose. Jerry thought she was cute.

"I'd *love* it. For one thing, I'd get away from my

little sister. You got a room of your own?"

"There's just me in my family. My mom's a singer. Professional. She's on tour now. That's why I'm staying with my grandma."

"No kidding?" Crystal looked at him with interest. "On tour? Wow! What's her name? Does she have records out?"

"*Quiet!* Class, form a group around me." Mrs. Craig rescued him before he figured out how to say his mom's tour was to a string of bars across North Dakota and Montana. "Class, this is Mr. Johnson. He's going to point out all the interesting things we'll want to remember from our trip today. I know you'll show Mr. Johnson how polite we all are at Washington School."

Mr. Johnson was small and skinny with a blond mustache. Jerry noticed him raise his eyebrows when she mentioned *polite*. Actually, though, except for a few guys jabbing their elbows into each other and people smirking at each other, the class shuffled from room to room almost quietly.

18

V

The first-floor exhibits were boring—cabinets full of platters and pitchers and red goblets. The sort of thing his grandma might like. And the picture gallery had a display of paintings with a lot of zigzags and dots. On the other hand, Jerry found himself looking more and more closely at the house itself. All the rooms had big double doors made out of dark wood. The ceilings were high and the rooms were huge, with tall windows and fireplaces. One room was mostly glass—an all-year-round garden with two palm trees and flowering plants.

Jerry tried to imagine what living here would have been like. It would be a great place for playing games. Even something simple like hide-and-seek. There were a thousand places to hide just on that one floor. Climbing the steps to the second floor, he thought how great the banister was for sliding down. Kids in here would have had a blast, if it wasn't turned into a place to tiptoe through being polite.

The second-floor exhibits were interesting—Indian clothes and weapons and a tepee you could see into to tell just how they lived. Even kids who'd seen it all a couple of times got into that section. Mr. Johnson explained everything and Jerry forgot about the eerie feeling he'd had when he came in.

They shuffled out of the Indian area behind Mr. Johnson to several smaller rooms. The first was a smallish room crammed with big furniture, dark wood, knobby with carving. The main chair had a tall back and stiff arms. It reminded Jerry of pictures he'd seen of electric chairs in prisons. The table had legs that bulged and coiled like snakes. A lamp shade drizzled fringe fat as worms. Crowded in, Jerry started to sweat.

"This is one of the few rooms in the museum which we have left untouched," Mr. Johnson explained. "It was the study of one of our area's most interesting figures—Mr. Ezekiel Gilchrist. Ezekiel Gilchrist was an early experimenter with electricity and magnetism. During the second half of the nineteenth century, a good deal of work was being done in those areas, and East Bent was the home of one of the more eccentric figures to be involved in those studies."

Mr. Johnson paused and pulled on his mustache, looking at them with a half smile. "How many of you like horror movies?" Almost the whole class raised their hands. Everybody stopped whispering and looked at him. "Mr. Gilchrist, who once lived in this house, was convinced that he could bring back the dead through electricity. I wouldn't swear to its being true myself, but back in his day, stories started to circulate that he was robbing graves for some of his experiments." Crystal looked at Jerry and rolled her eyes. "What we do know for sure is that he had some very strange apparatus built here and that he accumulated a big library on all that was known at the time about electricity, magnetism, mesmerism, and all related fields. Those books are still here."

"What's mesmerism?" Jerry was surprised to hear his own voice asking the question.

"Well, that was a complicated theory back at the time that said that there's a force called animal magnetism—a sort of electricity that flows through the human body and animates it. Mesmerism used that force, some experimenters claimed. Without that force, the theory was, you'd be dead. Ezekiel carried it a step further and was trying to prove that, with it, you could stay alive more or less forever. Or come out of your body and live again, at least partially, if you'd already died."

"Wooooh," somebody in the back said.

"Yeah," Johnson continued, "exactly. That's what people at the time thought. They thought the whole thing was creepy. Churches complained that he was going against God. Nobody trusted him. I guess that's why one day he just packed up and left."

"Where did he go?" Jerry hoped it was a long way away.

Johnson shrugged. "Nobody knows. He disappeared into thin air. Nobody saw him take the train. Nobody knew where he went. He left the house completely furnished. They looked for him, but to tell you the truth, I don't know how hard. Most of the town was glad to get rid of him. And since he left everything behind, the house and all the rest became the property of the town. That's how we got the museum."

"It was his house? He lived here by himself?" asked Angie, the red-haired girl who sat next to Jerry.

"In the end he did, for the last year or two. His brother had lived here with his wife and two children. The couple drowned in a tragic accident.

When the brother and his wife died, Ezekiel became guardian for the children. It's unclear what became of them. Gilchrist said they'd gone East to live with relatives, but after his disappearance, all attempts to trace them failed. The house would, of course, have been theirs if the city had been able to locate them."

"So they might come back and claim it? Throw the museum out?" one of the kids who never said anything in school piped up. Everybody was hanging on Mr. Johnson's story.

Mr. Johnson laughed. "I think we're safe now. They'd be over a hundred today. And if their descendants made a claim, I believe the time limit would be over—the town has a clear claim on the building today."

"Is anything left from when they were here? Anything of theirs?" a kid named Matthew asked while Jerry was swallowing, wondering the same thing. His throat was dry.

"Come next door. Not much was saved, but I'll show you what there is."

The next room was a jumble of furniture and knickknacks. It looked like an old-time yard sale. "We are rearranging the family possessions into a new display now," Mr. Johnson said. "Ezekiel Gilchrist's study was a higher priority since he was thought of as the Dr. Frankenstein of his day." He laughed, and most of the kids did, too. Jerry didn't. He shivered.

There was a small bed shaped like a sleigh and a brightly painted wooden train off in a corner. Dried flowers under glass domes, a gold watch in a case, a stiff-legged doll with a painted china head and long blond curls. The furniture was carved wood, but it didn't have the look of dragon tails and snakes the way the table in the other room had. Jerry looked around and started to relax.

"Downstairs, we have an album with photos of family members," Mr. Johnson told them. "Up here there's just this small picture of the two children I told you about. The ones who went back East and were never heard from." He held it up.

Jerry was in the front row. There was no way he could not look at the photograph, though he almost didn't. He looked at the floor and then back up quickly. The girl was there, with the fat shoulder-length curls. She had her hand on her brother's shoulder. He was smaller, looked maybe three or so. But it was the same boy. And the girl he would have known anywhere. Except she was smiling. When he'd seen her, she'd looked scared to death. Jerry swayed on his feet and swallowed hard.

"What, son?" Mr. Johnson was looking at him.

24

He must have said something or made some sort of noise, though Jerry couldn't remember that he had.

"Ghosts," he blurted out, turning red as soon as he had. "Has anybody ever said they saw ghosts here?"

Some kids snickered and Crystal looked at him funny. "Not that I know of," Mr. Johnson said kindly. "But it's true there've been reports over the years that people have heard something like a train whistle coming from inside at night." He smiled, pointing to the toy train in the corner. "Maybe that comes to life at night and chugs around the place. Other than that, no headless figures, no white sheets."

Mr. Johnson put the picture back on the table behind him. He was looking at the class gathered in front of him and didn't notice a folded piece of yellowed notepaper that had been on the table under the edge of the frame. In fact, nobody except Jerry saw the scrap of paper flutter off the edge of the table and float to the floor. Furtively, pretending to tie his shoe, Jerry bent over and palmed it. On the way out of the room, he pushed it into his jeans pocket.

VI

Being seen by the boy was terrible. That night Mattie made Edward stay in the basement of the tower, where they spent their days. Mattie couldn't forgive herself for letting Edward persuade her to leave early. What would Mama and Papa think? She was twelve. Her cousin Leticia had been married at fifteen. Mattie was almost a woman, old enough to mother Edward. But she had acted like a child.

Deep down Mattie knew that it hadn't been just Edward's pleading that had made her give in and fade through the wall so much too early. Mattie loved the autumn. She used to twirl and spin in the leaves the gardener had heaped by the back fence. Yellow and orange, they'd floated up in the air around her like butterflies. Mama always chided her for causing work for others.

Wonderful parties with her dance cards filled, a handsome husband . . . children. Those were her dreams twirling in the leaves. In the old life, each new season had filled her with dreams of her future. Each new autumn told her she was growing up.

But Mattie would never be older than twelve. Her days were always the same. She and Edward stayed in the lower room of Uncle's tower. At night they faded through to the old house. Time had stopped for them. Seeing the boy stirred feelings she'd almost forgotten. Thoughts about love. Mattie was a romantic. She'd hoped to be beautiful, like Mama. She'd imagined a tall, handsome man falling in love with her. The boy outside was close to her age. Did he think her pretty? Mattie glowed a little brighter, blushing. How foolish her thoughts were becoming. The boy was a pudgy little stump—one of the new people.

Normally her thoughts were mostly on the past, with the people who had gone on. Mama and Papa and Mattie's friends. What Edward dreamed of, those long days in the dim tower room, lit only by the shimmer their bodies had in the dark, what his thoughts were, she never knew. People all needed the privacy of their dreams.

Uncle Ezekiel's laboratory was up the ladder in the main part of the tower. He was there, eyes closed, rocking back and forth, soothed by the magnetic forces that washed over him. He did not mind being alone. All his life that's what he had wanted. After that horrible time, when Mama and Papa had drowned in the sailing accident and Uncle had been supposed to look after them, Mattie had seen clearly enough that he was not a suitable person to bring up Edward and her. He tried, pretending to be interested in the stereopticon that showed scenes of exotic places, because she and Mama had loved it, talking about trains to Edward the way Papa had. But he was clumsy in his efforts to be a parent and soon dropped them, leaving the care of Edward and the house to her and to Mrs. Kowalski, the Polish woman who was their cook.

What had happened to her and to Edward was not Uncle's fault. He had told them over and over to stay away from the tower. The only entrance was a tunnel whose opening was concealed under the large stone beside the carriage house. What he did there was secret, always, even before Mama and Papa had gone. But Uncle did not understand how little boys thought. He did not know that the more he warned Edward to stay away, the more his nephew would long to see his secret place.

The afternoon it happened would always stay sharp and clear in Mattie's mind—every detail.

Uncle had left his laboratory and gone to his study in the house. Planning to return at once, he had uncharacteristically left the tunnel entrance uncovered. In his study, he had found that one book led to another, and he must have been away from the laboratory for at least an hour.

Edward had been playing in the yard, trying to roll his hoop. Mattie had watched its wobbly progress over the cobblestone drive for a while and then had gone in to speak to Cook. When she'd returned, Edward was gone. At first she had looked around front for him, under the big spruce tree where he had his secret cave. But when she saw the stone standing out of place, Uncle's tower entrance gaping open, Mattie had turned ice-cold. Somehow, she had known in that instant that something awful had happened. As fast as she could, Mattie had stumbled through the dark tunnel, calling Edward's name. But her only answer was an ominous hissing from Uncle's laboratory ahead. Then there was a bitter smell of acid that Mattie would never forget.

Springing up the ladder, Mattie had burst into the tower room to see Edward holding on to an enormous wheel that was covered with twisted wires, a wheel that was humming and flashing green fire. "Edward!" she had screamed, and grabbed him. That was the last thing she remembered, reaching for Edward and pulling at him, then finding herself held fast and trembling, gripped by the electric force of Uncle's wheel.

Uncle had found them both like that. He had done what he could to save them, Mattie knew that was true. But it was too late; their bodies' lives were over. Still, Uncle and his wheel had managed to perform a miracle. Their inner selves had not gone on, as their bodies had, as Mama and Papa had. Uncle and the wheel had called them back.

"Soul and Spirit are Fraud!" That was Mattie's first memory, returning to the world when Uncle brought them back, the sound of his voice chanting, exulting over them. "The Electric is Life!" She could forgive his carelessness, leaving the stone ajar. What Mattie could never find it in her heart to forgive Uncle was his pleasure at the sight of the flimsy inner selves that were all that was left to her and Edward after that terrible afternoon. He had celebrated, the jowls to his heavy head quivering as he chuckled with delight, because they had proved his theory right.

VII

"*Magnus Magnes ipsum est globus.* 'The earth itself is a giant magnet.' Queen Elizabeth's physician said that—one of the great thinkers of all time. A forerunner of Ezekiel Gilchrist." Mattie could understand his bragging to her the way he often did. Uncle cared more about magnetism and the electric force than he did about anything else. He was a genius. What he had done, bringing Mattie and Edward back, keeping himself alive, feeding off the same force that had returned their inner bodies to life, had to be one of the most amazing achievements of all time.

She tried not to look at his eyes when he talked. His flesh was cloudy white, like Cook's blancmange, a quivery, pale gelatin. She wondered if he could ever guess how strange he looked, how awful. He was pale as a night-blooming plant, thin in the body but big headed, like an eerie blossom on a stem. He reminded her of the white sprouts she'd seen on Cook's potatoes, shut in the cellar all winter.

Since he seldom moved from his chair before the wheel, his body had become spindly from lack of use. Still, infused with electric force, he could move fast as a cat if an idea seized him. His domed head, fuzzed with gray like a dandelion gone to seed, inspired Mattie with a kind of awe. She cowered despite herself when he deliberately turned his massive head and fixed her in his lion's gaze.

Normal people would be more afraid of him than of her, and Mattie was what she used to call a ghost. Uncle Ezekiel had never been dead, but he looked like death.

Shielded by the web of magnetic forces his wheel spun about him, Uncle sat and thought. Occasionally he would still the wheel and move among his beakers and wires, testing an idea. His shoulders were erect, his body stringy and taut in his dingy, tattered shirt and shiny black trousers. The cloth was ripped and split and floated in rotten tags as he moved. As he sat before the wheel, within the invisible waves it sent forth, time stopped for him. Uncle Ezekiel had no human needs. He never ate nor drank nor went to the toilet nor slept.

Crouching in the room below the laboratory the

night after they had seen the boy, Mattie kept Edward beside her. She was terrified that Uncle would call them. Secrecy had been everything to Uncle from the very beginning. After she and Edward disappeared, suspicions were aroused. Mrs. Kowalski had told people that his story about their going back East was untrue. Officials had come to ask questions. The town had always feared and distrusted Ezekiel. Of course, they could find no reason to accuse him of anything.

Eventually, they stopped coming. But Uncle had been frightened; Mattie could see that. Afterward he had worked even harder in his laboratory, studying how to use the same forces that had brought her and Edward back to preserve himself. He wanted to hide himself away, to be free forever of outside interference. He spent five years trying, and then he learned how to stop time in the wash of magnetism from his wheel. Before the wheel, Uncle would always stay fifty-five years old, fifteen years older than Papa when he died. Ezekiel shut himself up in the tower. He wanted to go even further. He wanted to discover the secret of immortality itself. He wanted to free himself from the wheel, be alive forever, and keep his body as well. He did not want to be a shadow, Mattie reflected bitterly. Not for himself the life he'd condemned them to.

Now, the boy had seen them and if Uncle knew,

would he dissolve the flimsy lives she and Edward had left them? He'd become harder through the years, stranger. Nothing mattered to him but his quest for the secret to eternal life. He felt he was close; he could taste the fame and fortune that would be his once he'd pierced the greatest secret of all. Little as he cared about the company of others, still, that was what drove him: the moment when the world would have to acknowledge his genius, when the scientists who had called him a crank and a crackpot would have to bow to his superior talent.

Mattie and Edward could not hinder his progress. Nothing was sacred to Uncle but his quest. Their "bodies" were only images in the air. If they touched each other with both hands, the image would dissolve in a shower of sparks. Uncle had instructed them not to embrace. His wheel was also a danger to them; they had to maintain a distance from it. Taller than twice Uncle's height, covered with black-taped copper wires coiling like snakes, the wheel hummed as it spun, crackled and spat as the wires reacted to one another.

Suppose he knew about the boy? Would he decide she and Edward might give away his presence? Force him into the open before he was ready? But how could he know, shut inside the blind tower? Uncle's gifts were uncanny. Sometimes Mattie thought he could see through stone walls. Still, she waited through almost that whole night before any summons came.

"Cheeldrin!" Uncle Ezekiel's voice was raspy from lack of use. For a minute, Mattie thought of taking Edward's hand and running. But Uncle was the person who had replaced Mama and Papa. He "took care" of them. Without him they would be all alone. Edward following, with dread in her heart, Mattie floated up the ladder to Uncle's laboratory.

VIII

Uncle's laboratory was strangely silent. A few bubbles exploded and popped on the surface of acids in the beakers on the shelves lining the wall behind the wheel. Uncle had turned off the machinery, something he almost never did.

"Adjusting my electric overflow device." He nodded up toward the roof that soared far above them. "That is where the extra electric force flows. Without that to absorb the surges, the magnetotron would overheat and melt. There it is." He chuckled. "Right for all the world to see. If all the world were not too stupid to notice."

Following his gaze, Mattie saw a thick wire running all the way up to the peak of the tower roof and, evidently, through it. Vaguely, she recalled a weather vane—an iron bird that spun whether the wind blew or not. In the Before Time, she had wondered about it. Wondered why Uncle had slowly pulled himself up the ladder to adjust the bird's speed. Uncle was not athletic like Papa. She had shuddered at the screeching sound of metal against metal when it was going fast.

"How are you, Uncle?" She tried to sense his mood. He looked excited but not angry. More preoccupied. He had not seen the boy. He did not suspect she'd betrayed his secret. Mattie relaxed, and the pale glow of her body dimmed a shade or two. She dropped Edward's hand.

"Well, Martha, thank you. I am afraid I haven't always been the best of uncles, but I want you to know I'm always thinking of the two of you. All alone as you are." His words came slowly, his voice pebbly and dark. He pulled his gray eyebrows together like storm clouds. Edward caught Mattie's hand again.

"We are well. Thank you for your concern, Uncle."

"Perhaps I haven't been fair to you two. I have left you to pine away by yourselves for lo these years. Children need playmates." His expression did not reflect the kindness of his words. His eyes were not on them but fixed, as if he were seeing a vision all his own.

Mattie stared. All her attention was on Uncle. She should have been watching Edward.

Edward had heard the word *playmate*. He brightened. Before Mattie could stop him, he spoke. "We *saw* a real boy. And Mattie wouldn't let me talk to him. Mattie made him leave. Tell her, Uncle, I want a boy to play with."

Spots floated before Mattie's eyes. No one, *ever, ever,* was to see them. The room was a blur.

Uncle took two menacing steps toward them. "Out of the mouths of babes, eh, Mattie? Now I learn how far you are to be trusted."

She shrank toward the ladder. "It was my fault," she said. "Don't blame Edward. . . ." Then she stopped. Protecting Edward was wrong now. She could not leave him behind.

But Ezekiel stopped advancing. A gleam came into his eyes. "A boy, you say?" He turned to Edward, who was so frightened he glowed palely against the gloom from his uncle's beakers and tubes, the only light in the room.

"I'm sorry, Mattie," Edward whimpered. "You said . . . " His voice trailed off in a sob.

"Come, come," Ezekiel said. "Do I seem angry?" He sugared his voice and, with obvious effort, wrenched his lips into a smile. "You should have told me. That's all I meant."

"It only just happened, Uncle," Mattie said. "Yesterday."

"He saw you? And Edward?"

She nodded.

"He'll be back. Boys come back and back to sniff like puppies if something puzzles them. We shall have to think how to get him here alone . . . so you and he and Edward can play." He ran a hand, limp and clammy as a fish, through his spiky hair. He looked at them with a cagey glance.

Edward couldn't hold himself in. "I'd *love* a boy to play with. I *told* you, Mattie. We *ought* to have a boy to play with. See, Uncle's not so . . ." He stopped and rolled his eyes at Mattie, begging her not to be angry.

"Uncle takes good care of us, Edward. Haven't I always told you so?" Mattie spoke briskly. Whatever Uncle wanted, she would do it. Lure that boy to play with them. She would not worry about why Uncle Ezekiel wanted him. She had to look out for Edward and for herself. Let the outside boy take care of himself.

"He was alone, this boy? No one else saw you?" She nodded. "Well," Uncle Ezekiel said genially, "I think we should send him an invitation. The way your Mama and Papa did, you remember, for parties?" Uncle's heavy-lidded eyes widened in an attempt at joviality.

"But I don't know his name, Uncle. Or where he lives." He couldn't be telling her to start wandering about outside? She and Edward stayed inside the iron fence.

"He'll come back. Did he see you disappear? Through the wall?"

Mattie hesitated, then nodded, ashamed.

But he was delighted. "Perfect, my lambs. Perfect. Then he'll *have* to come back. You must be a mystery for him, don't you see? We shall have him here as easy as metal to a magnet."

"We'll be careful not to show ourselves again, Uncle. I've never let that happen before. Not in all this time. Just that once."

"Good. Yes. That's right. No need to draw in more. All I want to begin is one or two." He cleared his throat. "One or two children to come in of an evening, play with you and Edward. That would be pleasant, wouldn't it?"

Edward couldn't believe their good fortune. "Wouldn't that be grand, Mattie? I'd let the boy be the locomotive sometimes. He could have a turn and not *always* be the caboose." He looked wistful, already reluctant to turn loose his favorite role. Mattie had to smile. Her heart lifted. Was it possible Uncle really wanted them to have friends? That he'd thought of a way for them, strange as they were, to know a little again of the outside world?

"We shall leave a note," Ezekiel said. "Where we

know he will find it. Where only *he* will understand it, in case it goes astray. It may take more than one trial, but we'll have him here. You can count on it."

"I don't know where his house is," Mattie said.

"We'll leave it in *your* house," her uncle replied, looking smug. "He will come back here; he will go through the museum, trying to find a clue. To explain who you were, what happened to you that day."

His voice had deepened. It was almost gravelly. The tone warned her. But, still, the boy in the spectacles was no worry of hers. Sometimes Mattie could hate them all—the children she knew were out there, skipping rope, playing blindman's bluff and croquet on summer nights. Sledding and skating in the winters. All her friends had grown old and died. Why should she care about this new boy?

"Isn't there a photograph of you two still inside? The one your mama kept on her mantel?"

Mattie thought. "It's upstairs. In the small reception room. But now it's all a jumble of things from here and there. It's not a proper room anymore." She hated the way they'd scrambled the familiar house and turned it into something that wasn't theirs.

"That's where we'll put the note. The boy will come; he will be looking for something like that

41

little portrait. If we leave our note there, he will read it. I know boys. Brace up, little Edward. You shall have a new playmate before the week is out." Ezekiel Gilchrist turned his massive head toward them. Mattie was used to Uncle lost in the deep frown of thought. She felt chilled by the sight of his smile.

IX

Leaving the museum with the class, Jerry thought of what his grandma was always saying about his mom. "Money burns a hole right through her pocket." He felt that folded piece of paper, glowing red as a coal, bulging and calling attention to itself, hidden deep as it was in his pocket. He even had to make himself stop limping slightly, favoring that side.

Halfway down the sidewalk, he turned and looked back at the museum building, just like a magician's castle with its tower at one end and its odd-shaped windows and little sections of roof jutting up here and curving away there.

"How come we never get to go inside the tower?" Sean, Crystal's friend, asked Mrs. Craig just as Jerry came up to the bus.

43

"It's what was known as a blind tower," she replied. "There's no way into it. It's purely ornamental. Back then, people wasted a lot of space when they built their homes."

"A blind tower," Jerry repeated dumbly, looking back at it. The phrase had a menacing feel to it.

"*I'd* never do that," Crystal said. "The tower is where I'd want my room. I'd never build one with no doors or windows."

"Tastes change," Mrs. Craig said briskly. She was busy checking to be sure everybody had come out to the bus.

"Weird the way that weather vane keeps turning," Sean said. "I don't feel any wind."

"Muuumph," Mrs. Craig said. "Get on, everybody. We don't want to be late and make our mothers worry."

Jerry tried to imagine his mom worried if he was twenty minutes late. What kid had a mom home anyway? Climbing up the bus steps he looked back over his shoulder at the steep, peaked roof to the tower. Sean was right. The iron crow with its wings spread out was circling around and around. *Screeek, creak.* He heard the metal grinding.

Crystal, behind Jerry, bent down and looked, too. "Maybe there're air currents up high like that, different from what we feel down lower."

"That might be it," Sean said.

Jerry looked up at the tops of the tall evergreen trees, not much below the tower roof. They didn't stir. He got on the bus and didn't say anything. Crystal sat down beside him. He knew she was dying to ask him why he'd mentioned ghosts. But she was a little shy of him, coming from Minneapolis and having a mom who was a singer. Jerry didn't give her an in. No way was he talking to *anybody* about what he'd seen. How could he?

"You know those kids in the picture? The ones that would be more than a hundred now? I saw them. Day before yesterday. Fading through the wall to the tower." Sure. He could imagine what would happen if he came out with that. Crystal was starting to think he was possibly cool. After that, she'd figure he was just a liar. Especially since, Jerry thought, sighing in disgust, he had kind of led her to believe his mom's career was some kind of big deal. If he mentioned the ghosts, she'd write off everything he'd said and figure he was just a blowhard.

"That was an interesting museum," he said real quick, before she had a chance to ask him anything. "Only I thought for sure there'd be a couple of old ghost stories floating around about it. All it takes is a foggy night and somebody's sure to see that

Gilchrist guy slinking along the porch. Especially in a small town like this."

"I guess East Bent seems kind of tiny to you. After living in a big city and all. Did you meet a lot of cool people from your mom? Did you ever talk to Prince?"

"Once," Jerry said. "Just for a couple of minutes. He's a nice guy." Jerry had seen Prince being driven past once when he was waiting to cross the street. He and Clayton had waved and Prince had rolled down the window to his stretch limo and said, "You guys take it easy." Or it could have been another guy who looked just like Prince. They were reasonably sure it was him. "East Bent is pretty nice," Jerry continued. "I kind of like it being quiet and all."

Crystal made a face. "It's *too* quiet. Seriously. What was he like? Prince, I mean."

"Like I say, nice." Jerry shrugged. "Friendly. But he had to go someplace. I didn't see him for long."

"Has your mom ever toured with him?"

"She's more country-western. And she's just starting out." Jerry was starting to hate himself. Now he had Crystal thinking he was some kind of halfway famous person and tossing her long blond ponytail over her shoulder like she was dying to impress him. It would have been wonderful if he

46

hadn't known it could all come crashing down around his dumb jug ears.

And he had the scrap of paper in his pocket—the one that he was scared to death to open up. His mouth was dry and his ears were burning. It was too much. Boy, did he ever wish for Clayton.

After they'd piled off the bus and collected their stuff, Jerry acted like he had somewhere superimportant to go. He had to get somewhere alone and look at the paper. He ran the whole four blocks to Grandma's from school, which left him panting. Somehow, he couldn't bring himself to stop somewhere along the way, pull out the paper, and unfold it. He had to be *inside*, under a roof, hidden by walls before he touched that paper again.

Grandma had a part-time job cleaning the congregational church on Tuesday, Thursday, and Saturday afternoons, which meant he'd be alone for a couple of hours at least. That was important, too. He didn't want anybody around when he unfolded the paper.

X

Carefully fishing the paper from his pocket, Jerry
considered for the first time that it might not say
anything at all. It might be just a paper protecting
the table from being scratched by the picture frame,
something like that. It was fragile, a sheet of notepaper that had turned fuzzy from age. It was yellowed and brittle at the edges.

Jerry sat down on the bed in his mom's old room,
where he was staying at Grandma's. He smoothed
the paper open beside him. There was writing—in
a spidery, old-fashioned handwriting, in black ink.
The writing looked fresh, odd on the creamy old
paper.

To the boy outside our fence:
  We saw you by the gate. I know you

saw my brother and me. Don't be afraid.
Won't you be our friend? We would
never harm you. Hide and stay after they
lock the doors. After the others go. Then
we shall come to play with you. Please
be our secret friend. Don't tell others.
Don't spoil our game. You will be safe.
Believe us and come.

For a long time, five minutes or more, Jerry simply sat and stared at the paper, reading it over and over until the letters squirmed on the paper and stopped making sense. "Don't be afraid." Reading that, he shivered. "We would never harm you." "Believe us and come." The words had a sneaky feel sometimes when he read them, as if somebody were trying to lure him in. Then, the next time through, they could seem friendly. He remembered how frightened the girl had looked.

Were *they* in some kind of danger? Who were they? Was it a trick? What should he do? Suppose, just suppose, they *were* ghosts? Imagine if they *were* and Jerry was the person to discover them. And he could prove it, not just blab on about how he'd seen one, the way people usually did. Borrow Grandma's camera and take pictures. Talk them into going public, with him to make all the arrangements, of course. Can you imagine the TV shows that would be panting to have the three of them?

"No, I wasn't afraid," Jerry imagined himself explaining. "I suspected right off that they wouldn't hurt anybody. And I figured you have to take a few chances once in a while." He'd say that with a smile, so it wouldn't look like he was bragging or anything. Was there really, when you came right down to it, any reason to think ghosts would be out to hurt people? Jerry figured that, after all, suppose he had died and come back. Wouldn't it make sense to think that he'd still be just as nice as he was before? Wouldn't it seem likely that people would come back the way they were? In which case, even if the children he'd seen were ghosts, wouldn't they probably be harmless?

He remembered again how scared the girl had looked and he shivered, despite all his reasoning with himself. Still, how many chances does a person get to do something that will make him a household word? Wouldn't his mom feel bad about dumping him once he showed up on the cover of *People* magazine? Jerry rolled over on his back and stared at the cracks in Grandma's ceiling, leaned up on his elbow and followed the flowers on the vines on the wallpaper, gazed unseeing out the window beside the bureau, not noticing that it was getting

50

darker and time for Grandma to return.

"Dreaming away in here, are you?" Grandma switched on the light and nearly scared Jerry out of his wits. He twitched upright, blinking at her. He must have had a wild look on his face, because she looked startled. "You haven't picked up a bug somewhere?" She came over and felt his forehead. "Cool as a cucumber. That's good. You come on out to the kitchen and help me get dinner."

"I'll be right there." He went to the bathroom and splashed water on his face. He dried his face, being careful to fold the towel straight again.

Grandma was frying bacon to go with their beans. Jerry got out the plates and silverware.

"Do you believe in ghosts, Grandma?" He carefully made sure his back was to her, setting the table, when he asked the question. "I saw something in the paper at the grocery store about a woman who saw her children two years after they were killed in a car crash. Standing in their family room."

"I don't know, Jerry. I try to keep an open mind."

"You mean you really think it's possible?"

"Well, don't be so quick to say this or that is impossible, that's all I'm saying. Not everything that people claim happens does, that is clear. But that's not to say that odd things don't occur sometimes. I don't believe in jumping to conclusions either way.

On the whole, I'd say perhaps that lady *wanted* to see her children and that's why she did. Maybe it was just shadows she saw, who's to say? But I'd never be the one to say for sure that there's not something out there more than we know."

Jerry poured himself a glass of milk. What she said made sense, if you wanted to look at it that way.

After supper, scraping the plates, Jerry was still waffling this way and that about what he should do. As he dropped the silverware into the dishwasher basket, Grandma said, "Jerry, you think you can heat your dinner in the microwave on Saturday? I'll be at church until nine at least. They've got two weddings back-to-back and I'll want to have everything set for their Sunday service." Grandma went to the Full Gospel Temple and wouldn't want to be busy in another church on Sunday morning.

"Oh, sure, Grandma. I use ours all the time when Mom's not around. No problem." Jerry heard the tremble in his voice, if Grandma didn't. He turned ice-cold and froze, one hand on the counter, until she did look at him funny.

"This is your day for space travel, I believe. You've been getting that dreamy look all evening."

"I'm okay," Jerry said. The museum closed at five on Saturdays, the same as every other day. He'd read the notice on the door. Grandma was just handing him four hours when nobody would look for him or wonder about where he was. Jerry felt it had to be a sign.

"Do you believe that things are kind of arranged ahead? That maybe some things you were meant to do?" Jerry snapped the plastic clip back on the bread wrapper and put the loaf in the fridge.

"This is your night to be the philosopher, Jerry. You're full of questions. You're thinking about your mom, aren't you? The way she's just *had* to try her luck with this music business come what may. Well, I think you're right. There are just some times when we have to explore, take our chances."

Jerry pushed the ON button and listened to the swish and hum of Grandma's dishwasher starting up. Grandma had helped him get his thinking straight. Even if they were talking in two different directions. He was meant to do what the note said.

That night in bed, Jerry imagined himself in the huge old mansion. Jerry thought of all the apartments he and his mom had lived in—none for more than a year or two. They were all places to pass through. The museum house was a place to be swallowed up in. A house that could hold all the private dreams and projects and plans that anybody could possibly imagine, even somebody who daydreamed a lot like him. Like Ezekiel Gilchrist, who had lived there a hundred years ago. "Yeah," he murmured into his pillow, "in a house like that, you'd start to think anything at all was possible."

XI

That Saturday afternoon, when he went to the museum, Jerry wasn't totally sure he'd stay. He was still teetering this way and that. He went back up to the cluttered room on the second floor to look at the picture another time. Hardly anybody was in the museum and the ones who were stayed in the Indian exhibits. He almost felt he was already alone as he stood looking at the photograph of the two smiling children.

Then, nervous, he looked for the men's room. He'd gone just before he left Grandma's. Now he had to again. In the bathroom, without really thinking about it, he realized that he was in the perfect place to hide. He could just sit in a booth with his feet up. In a little town like this, nobody would go pushing doors and checking. Again, it seemed like fate. He hadn't decided; it had kind of just come to him.

One reason the men's room was right was that it was new—added to the museum house itself. Hiding in here, he was in the museum and yet he wasn't. This was modern, with its shiny fixtures, cold tiles, and dark wood booths. Even so, after fifteen minutes, the bathroom turned out to be one of the spookiest rooms Jerry had ever seen. He didn't turn the light on, of course, and the only window was high and frosted. The light outside was getting dim anyway.

The pipes gushed and breathed and made tiny pinging noises. Once a man came in and flushed a urinal. Jerry watched his feet in their brown loafers. It could have been Mr. Johnson. Jerry breathed slowly, slowly, slowly. After the man left Jerry burst out with a desperate sneeze. The shadows grew darker and darker. Forty-five minutes to go to five. He fingered Grandma's small camera, which he'd tucked into his jacket pocket, and reminded himself why he'd come. This was his big chance. If he ducked out now, took off like a scared rabbit, he might never be famous.

He heard voices echoing distantly from the hall outside. People saying good-bye for the day. He heard the *briing* of the shop cash register around the corner as the woman cleared it. Footsteps and the click of the door. Cars starting. Then, eventually, quiet. A quiet like his grandma's spidery knit afghan settled over everything, a quiet Jerry could almost feel over his face, numbing him. The bathroom was almost dark. He put his feet on the floor and stood up, stiff. He snapped back the lock on his stall, starting at the sharp sound in the emptiness.

Wincing at the creak of the door, he stepped out into the empty corridor and looked around him. He walked down the hall to the front entrance and stood just inside the door. There was a snap lock that he could release from inside to dash out if he needed to. The window on the stair landing glowed peach, violet, and gold from the sunset, but the house was all shadows. Past the picture-gallery rooms to the left was the blind tower. It was that way Jerry looked, his hand resting on the door lock, his heart thudding.

In the dimness of the farthest room, the air by the wall began to glow faintly. Jerry almost thought he was wrong and he blinked his eyes to clear them. Then they were there—the two of them. The tall girl with the fat curls to her shoulders and the little boy, holding hands and looking across the rooms that separated them to stare in wonder at him. Jerry swallowed hard. His knees turned to water.

XII

"Mattie, the boy's here. The normal boy has come!"
Edward dashed ahead, through the galleries, Mattie
behind him. Mattie glanced down, smoothing the
folds of her dress, foolishly, since, like the rest of
her, her clothes never changed. She might as well
have touched a mirror, smoothed the hair of her
image in the shiny glass. The dress moved with her,
her curls bounced with the swing of her head, but
then they returned to their former folds.

"Edward! Mind your manners. You know better.
Remember what I told you."

The little boy pulled himself up abruptly, dancing
like a reined-in pony. "How do you do," he said in
a clear, piping child's voice. "I am Edward Gilchrist.
This is my sister, Mattie. Welcome to our house."
He looked around at Mattie to be sure he'd done
it right. She smiled approval.

"We are glad you could come," she said.

"It was nice of you to invite me," Jerry said, feeling dazed, as if he were in a dream. "My name is Jerry. Jerry Roberts. Do you live here at night?"

"We come when the people go," Mattie said carefully. Uncle would not want him asking about the tower.

"I never saw a normal boy before," Edward said, walking around Jerry and staring. "I don't *remember* any. Mattie is all I ever see. Your clothes are funny."

"Edward!" Mattie felt her face glow a little brighter. "You are being rude." She felt more embarrassed because she, too, had been trying not to stare at the boy's clothes. His pants were blue cloth, like farmers wore, only tight—his limbs were clearly outlined.

"That's okay," Jerry said. "I guess you're used to old-timey things." He was wearing jeans, a sweatshirt, and a nylon jacket. He had on running shoes. They were what Edward was staring at hardest. "I guess you don't have plastic and that sort of stuff."

"What's plastic?" Edward stooped to admire Jerry's bright shoes from closer up.

"You see the sides here, and the tips on the laces," Jerry said, leaning over the boy. "On your shoes, things like that would be leather or metal; on mine, they're plastic. It's something people make in factories. Out of oil, I think. They make lots of stuff out of plastic now." He felt foolish, realizing he didn't really know much about it. "See, let me show you." Jerry reached out to take Edward's arm, to guide him to touch the shoe. Little kids liked to feel things.

"*No!*" Mattie rushed forward. "Don't touch him!" But it was too late. Jerry's hand went through Edward's shoulder in a shower of tiny sparks.

"Agggghhhhh!" Jerry jumped back, holding his hand. It stung and then went numb. Edward's shoulder for a few seconds had a gaping hole through it, where Jerry's hand had been. Jerry ran his tongue around his mouth. There was a metallic taste, as if the dentist had been drilling against a tooth. He smelled a burnt smell.

"Sorry," Mattie said stiffly. "You can't touch us, you see." She held out her hand to Edward, who took it, looking frightened.

"I'm sorry, Mattie," Edward moaned. "I didn't touch the boy. I didn't mean to hurt the boy."

"No, Edward, that's all right," she comforted him. "You didn't do anything wrong. The boy didn't know. The boy has to learn how to play with us."

"I'm okay, Edward," Jerry said. "Like Mattie

says, it was my fault. Are you all right?" His arm tingled, feeling coming back. Jerry sensed from the formal way that Mattie apologized, from the rigid way she held herself, that she was embarrassed.

"He'll be fine," Mattie said. "We don't have normal bodies, you see." Her voice dipped so low over the last sentence that Jerry had trouble hearing her.

"Are you ghosts, then?" Jerry hated himself the minute he blurted out that question. Mattie looked betrayed.

"*Ghosts?*" Edward gasped. "Is that what we are, Mattie?"

"In a way," she said soothingly, all her attention on her brother. Jerry was afraid she'd never speak to him again. "We are the body's image. You know, when Cook makes jelly, she pours it into a mold? Then, when it sets, she shakes it out, all shining and sparkling, onto a plate?" Edward nodded, his eyes big. "Well, what we are, really, is like the mold. All bodies have a mold that keeps them who they are. Just the way Cook's heart shaped the jelly."

"I see what you mean," Jerry said. "You're saying we have this pattern that's programmed in. Something electric." His arm still tingled.

"Programmed?" Mattie was bewildered. She knew how to talk to Edward. She was beginning to despair of making sense of this new boy.

61

"That's the way we talk now," Jerry said quickly. "It means what you said. Just a different way of saying it. Not as pretty," he added shyly, hoping he could make her feel better. As soon as he'd seen her walking toward him, smoothing her skirt and looking away, Jerry had liked Mattie. She looked just the way he'd felt going into the new class the first day, afraid people would think he was different and laugh. "Your house is really beautiful." Later, when he knew her better, he could find out more about how they came to be the way they were. About what happened to their uncle.

"We play here," Edward said, happy enough again. "Have you ever played train?"

"I haven't. But if you show me how, I'll be glad to play with you."

Mattie unbent a little. The boy was kind. His speech was a little strange, and his clothes were outlandish. But he was not making fun of them and he was nice to Edward. She thought she might like Jerry.

"You run along the track and whistle and blow and stop," Edward explained excitedly. "The person who is the locomotive decides where the track goes. Sometimes you come to a tunnel." He frowned. "But you won't be as good as Mattie and me at tunnels."

"We could use the upstairs hall for a tunnel," Mattie suggested.

"I could drape sheets over a table or something," Jerry offered. "Did you ever play that way?"

"You could make caves?" Edward's eyes danced. "You can pick up things?"

"Can't you?" Jerry was surprised. Edward shook his head.

"But we go through them," he bragged. "Normal boys have to use doors. Mattie told me. And I remember. From the Before Time. Almost."

In the end, they worked out a game using their opposite talents. Edward and Mattie were as enchanted by Jerry's ability to lift their toys and make them work as Jerry was by their skill at fading through walls. Edward stared entranced when Jerry pulled his wooden train along the floor. Mattie wanted him to straighten the ribbon in her old doll's hair. She'd stopped playing with dolls long ago in the Before Time, but she had not liked seeing Charlotte with her crumpled bow. All of them did play train, and they let Edward be the locomotive the whole time. Mattie caught herself over and over looking at Jerry and smiling, sharing amusement at Edward's enthusiasm.

Finally, Mattie and Jerry were sitting together on the stair landing, watching Edward chugging around and around below them, talking about their lives like old friends. Mattie talked about the Before Time. Little things lying about the house reminded her, and she rattled on. The case in the corner held her mama's sewing implements. Mattie told him about learning to cross-stitch. She even confessed how she had hated sewing.

"My samplers came out all wrong," she sighed. "Mama never framed any of mine."

"Girls don't do that anymore," Jerry said. "They dress like boys and all—wear jeans like this." He stuck out one leg. Mattie marveled, trying to imagine it. Some girls had been wearing divided skirts, but Mama had thought them coarse. She wasn't sure she could ever wear anything like Jerry's pants—out in public. But still . . . never to have to sew . . .

"You must have a wonderful time," she said, dazzled by his plastic shoes and talk of machines with pictures that spoke and moved.

"It's not necessarily all that great," Jerry said. He told her about how his mom had gone off and left him for her tour, shipped him to East Bent where he didn't know anybody except his grandma.

"Your father allows this?" Mattie was bewildered, even more so when Jerry explained that his father lived with a different family, that many children had parents with two families and lived with one sometimes and the other at other times.

They found each other so sympathetic that they sat and talked and smiled and sighed. Jerry thought Mattie was more beautiful and delicate than any girl he'd ever seen. Playing train, he'd felt the camera in his pocket and blushed. Somehow it seemed wrong to think of snapping her picture. Seeing how shy she was, how nervous about being different, he wanted to protect her. She was so perfect, all her curls so even and shiny, her eyes flashing with that special glow she and Edward had. Jerry didn't feel half as nervous around her as he did with Crystal, where he was always laughing too loud or tripping over his feet. With Mattie, he knew he was the only boy friend she had. He thought he could lie down at her feet and worship her, she was so beautiful. For now, he pushed away his dreams of being famous. That could wait until Mattie wasn't so shy around him.

He wanted to ask about her uncle, the man Mr. Johnson had told them about. But somehow he felt that would be wrong, would upset Mattie. She'd told him about her parents drowning in an accident. Talking about that had been hard for her. He sensed that if he had pressed to know about Ezekiel Gilchrist, she would have had to talk about how she and Edward had been turned into ghosts. Look how she'd reacted when Edward had said something about that—nearly jumping out of her skin. Another time, when he knew her better, she'd tell him more. They'd already arranged that he'd come back next week. That would be plenty of time to think about persuading them to let him introduce them to the world.

At eight forty-five Jerry hated to leave.

"We'll look forward to seeing you soon," Mattie said formally as he was leaving. She was bashful again, afraid of how sorry she was to see him go.

"It was fun meeting you both," Jerry said, suddenly shy himself. "I'll be back next Saturday."

"Good-bye, Jerry!" Edward was cheerful again. "I *like* you." Mattie and Jerry laughed together at that as he let himself out the door.

XIII

As soon as the door clicked shut behind Jerry, Mattie forestalled any comments from Edward by bubbling on and on about how wonderful the evening had been. But her voice had a tinny sound that even Edward had to sense.

"What's the matter, Mattie? Didn't you *like* Jerry?" He caught her hand and peered up into her face, puzzled.

"Yes," she said truthfully. "I did like Jerry. And isn't it wonderful that he'll be coming back so soon to see us again?" She knew the smile she'd arranged her face into wasn't going to fool Edward. "I guess I feel a little sad, too, though, Edward. I suppose seeing a normal boy like Jerry starts me remembering the Before Time. You know how I sometimes feel sad, remembering the Before Time?"

Edward sighed and nodded, a concerned look on his face. He hated it when Mattie was sad. It scared him. Mattie was his protector. Mattie made everything all right.

"Let's go back upstairs," Mattie said in a brisk voice. "You might look at your train some more. Remember how Jerry pulled it for you?" She knew how to distract him. Soon Edward had forgotten to notice her and was engrossed in running from one place to another upstairs.

Mattie went back to the hall stairs, where she'd sat with Jerry. Her mood was hard to define. For two or three hours she'd let herself be a girl again. Edward's question about being a ghost had been like a bucket of ice water dashed in her face. Now that she knew Jerry, Mattie could no longer think of him just as one of the new people. Now she had to face what Uncle was asking her to do. Uncle was not having them invite Jerry back so that they would have a playmate. Edward could believe that readily enough, but Mattie knew better.

Uncle had a new theory. He had figured out a new way to use his magnetotron to try to get himself to live forever and keep his body just as solid as it was now. That was the goal of all his musings and trials; Mattie knew that well enough. He was not satisfied to have to sit before the machine to keep time from passing. He wanted to make his body new, to free himself to move about.

For all these years, she'd followed the course of his experiments by observing his moods. Three times before, he'd been excited the way he seemed to be now but soon had plunged into deep gloom that lasted for weeks. Outside the magnetic web spun by the wheel, Uncle would grow older like anyone else. She knew he had found his last idea would not work. Now, clearly, he had a new theory.

And clearly, he wanted to try it out. She knew, didn't she, that Uncle wanted Jerry to test what the magnetotron would do to him before he tried it on himself? Mattie tried to reason with herself, to find a way to see that what Uncle was planning was not so bad. Jerry had a chance of being the first person in history to live forever, never getting older. If everything worked all right, he would have a body as well, which was certainly more than she and Edward had been left with. There was some chance he might be left the way they were, she supposed. And some, she had to admit with a shudder, that he would not live through Uncle's trial.

If Uncle knew the machine would do what he wanted, he would not be trying it on someone else. Their accident had given him a chance to watch them and see the effects. Perhaps if the accident had never happened, Uncle would not have pursued this mad dream he had of becoming immortal. Mattie knew he would never have thought of using a living person to experiment on, back then in the Before Time. All these years and years alone in his laboratory had changed Uncle, made him more sure that whatever he wanted was right.

He was always strange, Uncle, always kept to himself. But when Mama and Papa were alive, Uncle had followed rules, washed for dinner, combed his hair. Afterward, he'd moved farther away from other people, slept in his laboratory on the stone floor, eaten at odd times. Cook muttered about him in those days. Mattie had tried to smooth her temper, telling her that Uncle was a genius who had to do things differently from other people. Mama and Papa used to tell her that, although they did keep trying to persuade Ezekiel to come to parties at the house, to be among people more.

Now, Uncle was far past considering anyone's rules but his own. He would do almost anything, sacrifice anybody, for the sake of his experiments. Eventually, he would order Mattie to bring Jerry, unsuspecting, to the tower. She *knew* that, Mattie admitted, leaning so far forward on her knees that the curls met in the front and curtained her face. She knew it, and she had been pretending to herself that she didn't. Telling herself that she did not care what happened to the new people, that it was no concern of hers.

Now she knew Jerry. The way he looked at her, Mattie could tell he admired her. And, now that she had seen him up close, Jerry no longer seemed so chubby. She was beginning to feel she liked men who had some flesh on their bones; they looked strong. His brown eyes flashed when he laughed; she smiled, remembering. He was a little short now, but he would grow. She thought of Jerry at sixteen, tall and muscular, with his blond hair trimmed just to his shirt collar. She could persuade him to wear trousers a little more elegant than the blue cloth ones he had had on tonight.

He would come to the house to see her, faithful and loving. He would bring her white roses, the way Papa had for Mama. He would help Mattie take care of Edward—they would become a little family. Mattie sighed and closed her eyes, her long lashes sweeping her cheeks. She was being a silly. That's what Papa would say. She knew it was a dream. That's why her voice sounded so tinny to Edward when she tried to talk to him about Jerry. She could not permit Jerry to keep coming. She had to warn him away. She knew that was the only right course.

XIV

"Your dinner okay?" Grandma hung up her coat on the entryway hook.

"Good. Great." Jerry tried to remember back before he'd left for the museum. What had he eaten?

"That stew always reheats good," Grandma said, smiling and settling into the armchair across from him. "I hadn't figured you for a Lawrence Welk fan." Jerry had switched on the TV as soon as he had come in, twenty minutes ago. He had just let it make noise and fill up the emptiness while he sat and tried to think about where he had been.

Confused, Jerry looked at the screen full of women whirling and dipping in puffy dresses. "I was waiting for another show," he said lamely.

"You must be missing your friends." His grandma untied her shoes and massaged her feet.

"Staring into space so much lately. Still, Jerry, you've got to give East Bent a chance. You might find out there's more excitement here than it looks like at first. Takes everybody a while to make new friends, that's all."

"It seems pretty exciting already," Jerry said. "And I've met some interesting people."

"Well, good. I'm glad to see you looking on the bright side. I always thought Cathy would be better off moving back here. After she and your dad split up, I hoped you'd both come home. But I guess she's just not ready."

"Mom wants a chance to make it. She doesn't think she'd get that here."

Grandma sighed. "Always greener on the other side of the fence. That was your mom from day one. A real firecracker, that one."

Jerry heard the pride in his grandma's voice while she pretended to run his mom down. She was hoping his mom would be a star. His grandma bought *People* magazine and those grocery store papers about famous people's divorces just like his mom did.

"She figures this may be her big chance."

Sometimes Jerry pretended to think his mom was dumb for chasing her dream the way she was. Deep down, though, he hoped, too. He wanted to be the kid of a famous singer. Have people all over look at him the way Crystal had on the bus. And he wanted Mom to make it. He loved the way her voice would thin out and then go full again. The way she'd lean into the sound and toss her long hair back, looking out over the audience's heads at the dream she was weaving with her music.

"Others have done it with less talent. Far less talent. I wanted Cathy to put in for Miss East Bent. Couldn't persuade her to try out. I believe she would have been Miss Wisconsin that year. Heaven knows where she might be today if she had listened to her mom."

Jerry stretched out on Grandma's sofa and covered himself with her afghan. Even the dippy-sounding music from the TV, like swirls of sticky syrup, relaxed him. He wanted to put off thinking about where he'd been, what he was going to do next. In Grandma's living room, with her rubbing her feet and sipping coffee across the room, Jerry was safe. There weren't any ghosts or even thoughts of ghosts that seemed right in that room with the TV going.

In bed, though, it was a different story. Jerry had barely brushed his teeth because he couldn't stand the sight of his reflection in the bathroom mirror. He expected it to say something, to reach out from the glass and electrocute him. Heart racing, he'd rinsed off his toothbrush and darted out the door, jumped in bed, and pulled the covers up to his ears.

He closed his eyes and saw Mattie's face, her large brown eyes and warm smile. Her delicate eyebrows and sweeping dark lashes. She was the prettiest girl he'd ever seen—even prettier than Crystal. And he'd talked to her more easily than he'd ever talked to any other girl.

Suppose they did come out of the museum and let people know about them? Then would Mattie still be a good friend of Jerry's? His special friend?

Jerry found himself feeling one way one minute and another the next. "You scooped *everybody*, kid." Jerry could still hear people saying that, see himself with "The Ghost Children" on the covers of all the magazines and newspapers on the rack. See job offers pouring in. Maybe he'd be a TV journalist—one of the ones who explore strange mysteries every week, open up vaults and dive to sunken ships and all.

But after he dreamed those dreams for a few minutes, he remembered how kind of delicate Mattie was—like an animal that lived deep in the woods. She looked at him with those big dark eyes, full of worries, and he felt tender toward her. He'd never felt that way before. He wanted to protect Mattie from people's thinking she was strange and he wanted to be with her.

He found himself wondering if it wouldn't be possible to have a girlfriend, a wife even, whom you just kind of worshiped from a distance, just sat and admired?

There would be something wonderful about that sort of love, he decided. So pure. That seemed nice. Better than his mom and her boyfriends smooching and worse. He and Mattie could lie in bed together, side by side, and talk and feel closer and closer.

"Jerry, you are giving up everything for me." He could hear Mattie's gentle voice, loving but sad, years from now if she became his secret wife. "Everybody must wonder why you don't have a flesh-and-blood wife, a normal family, a good-looking man like you. Don't your friends wonder why you never go out with them at night? Don't you miss having a *real* girlfriend?"

"Nobody could be more real to me than you, Mattie," Jerry would whisper, leaning close to her satin smooth cheek, breathing in the air just above her shiny brown curls. He scrunched down under the blankets, feeling how great he was, how fine it would be to dedicate his life to keeping Mattie and Edward safe. "And all I want in life is to protect you and Edward."

The more Jerry thought about it, the more he wondered if the way to go wasn't the quiet way. Did he have to brag on to the rest of the world? Really, wasn't the decent thing to protect Mattie and Edward and keep their secret? Couldn't he wait at least? Jerry couldn't quite turn loose all his hopes. But calling Mattie and Edward *ghosts* in front of the whole world—the thought of that was starting to make him shrink. Maybe later, when Mattie was more used to everything, when he'd had a chance to bring her more up-to-date. One thing he knew— he could never do anything to make Mattie feel weird or stared at. Jerry finally drifted off to sleep, feeling closer to noble than he ever had in his life before.

XV

Mattie felt like an animal in a trap. Every way her
thoughts took her, she banged against a wall. She
and Edward could run away. Leave the house and
sneak off—hide far away from their uncle. But no.
The idea of leaving their own house where everything was familiar and loved—where everything reminded her of their Before Time—made her dizzy.
Outside, what would they be? Ghosts. Jerry had
said it. People would scream and run from them.

Suppose, though, she tried to talk Edward into
the idea that it would be fun to go out into the
world and terrify everybody? He'd love glimmering
around like a firefly and fading through some sleeping child's wall to scare him senseless. Mattie could
even imagine herself taking pleasure in calculating
ways to startle a few people.

Were there still teachers out there who rapped you across the knuckles if you blotted your copy work the least little bit? Girls like Amanda Buckley who preened and prissed and looked at you sideways if your dress didn't come from Chicago?

Oh, yes, Mattie could imagine the look on the faces of a few people like that. Could even see herself making "Wooooh" ghost noises like the wind under the door, screeching like rusty nails and then floating down from the ceiling or, even better, up from the cellar. She could have sent Amanda Buckley shrieking out into the street in her curlpapers and her shift. Sent Miss Jubal Pomeroy bolting from her outhouse. Jerry could help them choose victims.

But what was the problem? Edward. Frightening people was one thing. Accidently killing them was something else. If she or Edward touched anybody with two hands, they would surely die. Uncle explained that their bodies had held in the electric force, the way wrapping does on wires. Jerry had felt an awful jolt just laying one hand against Edward. Without their outside bodies, Uncle said, they were like uninsulated wires—pure electric force.

"Animal magnetism—the life force," he'd exulted. "Others have searched for it. The great Paracelsus named it. But you and Edward are the first to display it. Through you I have proved how right

I was. Soul and Spirit are Fraud! The Electric is Life!" He had wavered to his feet in a lumbering dance, stiff from years and years of hardly moving.

Perhaps it would be better to go on, to be with Mama and Papa and all Mattie's friends, not caught here in between. Mattie had made her peace with their fate. She and Edward were outside the world, dreaming of the past. What went on beyond the spiked iron fence no longer concerned her. But Uncle's bringing Jerry in had changed everything. Now even Edward was startled into questions she'd carefully kept him from thinking of. *Ghosts. Ghosts.* Once the word was spoken there was no escaping it.

She and Edward were between two worlds. Where did they belong? Uncle was forcing her to meddle where she never wanted to, with the new people. She had to tell him about seeing Jerry. Uncle was too clever. He would never believe her if she said he had not come. Edward would never understand why she was lying. He would give her away for sure.

Mattie knew she couldn't feel, but even so her head throbbed.

After an hour that seemed endless, she spoke to Edward. "Let's go see Uncle, Edward. Tell him about Jerry coming." Edward looked at her suspiciously. He was smart. He knew she was frightened. But he was too little to unravel her thoughts. Feeling left out made him sulk.

"You go. I'll stay here." He knew the rule. She did not like to leave Edward alone.

"Edward." She was startled at how close her voice came now to sounding just like Mama's. Edward had been floating stretched out a few feet off the floor. He turned right side up and walked toward Mattie. He looked at his feet, not at her. "It's not my fault," she felt like screaming. "It's not my fault!" Sometimes she came close to grabbing him, to dissolving them both. At this moment she wavered, leaning toward him. Then she held out her hand and Edward took it. Together they floated up the spiral stairs to Uncle's laboratory.

The wheel was spinning, a silver blur against the greenish light from the bubbling vials of acid on the shelves along the wall. "Uncle." Mattie spoke distinctly, knowing he was in a kind of trance when the wheel was going so fast. "Uncle, we have news."

The magnetotron slowed. The humming and crackling of the wires faded to a lower pitch. His eyelids were closed at first, seemed stuck shut as they bulged from his lion's face. But when his eyes slid open, his gaze was sharp.

"The boy was here," he said gleefully. Mattie shivered.

"He's nice," Edward insisted. "Mattie doesn't like him all that much. But I say he's nice."

"You are mistaken, Edward," she said. "I never said Jerry wasn't nice." She had never felt lonelier or more hopeless.

"Well, that is grand. Everybody likes the little friend Uncle's found for you." Ezekiel smiled, rubbing his hands together.

"When is he coming back?" His red-rimmed eyes fixed on Mattie's.

"Next Saturday, Uncle. That's the only time he can come without causing notice."

"All right. He likes you, then? You and Edward?"

She nodded. "We are friends." She felt a stone inside her.

"Suppose . . . " Uncle's words were honeyed, dripping from his lips like syrup. "Suppose you two bring him through the tunnel and into my laboratory? I should like to be introduced to your new friend."

Even Edward was surprised by that. "Here, Uncle? But you always said nobody . . . " He stopped, embarrassed. He remembered how he hadn't listened, that time so long ago.

"I shouldn't shut myself off all the time, should

82

mix and mingle occasionally. You recall your mama used to insist on that, back in the old days." He chuckled in a way that was supposed to reassure them.

But Mattie remembered Uncle at a soiree Mama had given, hiding himself behind the heavy drapes in the drawing room, resting his cheek against the cold glass. He preferred the leathery bats that swung in the dimness high in the rafters of the tower to any human company. She felt his keen gaze boring into her.

"I can count on you, then. You will bring your new friend to be introduced on Saturday evening next?"

"Sure!" Edward exclaimed enthusiastically. There was a long pause.

Mattie felt Uncle Ezekiel relax as, eventually, she nodded.

XVI

By Tuesday, Jerry had walked past the museum fifteen times. Knowing Mattie and Edward were floating inside the tower made his heart beat faster. That wasn't any kind of life for a nice little kid like Edward. And a beautiful girl like Mattie shouldn't spend year after year in a dismal stone tower. Wouldn't she get a kick out of watching MTV with him some afternoon after school? It'd blow her mind.

Actually, that might be a little too much so soon. Maybe he ought to check out some tame movies to watch on Grandma's VCR—stuff like *The Wizard of Oz*. How about *E.T.*? The extraterrestrial might make her and Edward feel a little less weird. And kids in the movie were flying the way Mattie and Edward could.

There had to be a way to sneak her out some of the time, so she'd know a little of what the world was like. He'd keep her and Edward a secret. Remembering the way everybody had laughed when he'd mentioned ghosts on the class trip, Jerry let himself for just a few seconds waver toward letting some kids from class in on it. Crystal and Sean, at least. But he saw right away that was impossible.

He blushed remembering the braggy stories he used to make up with him saving people and all that. The crowd applauding at the end. Knowing Mattie had made him feel different. Sure, maybe it would be fun to be famous and all. But those quiet moments sitting on the steps with her, with Mattie's shining eyes looking so amazed when he told her about the outside world and so trusting when she told him about her parents and all—those moments were more special than anything he'd imagined, thinking of crowds clapping.

By Wednesday, Jerry knew he was in love. He'd liked girls before—Crystal, for instance. And he still did think she was a nice girl for a friend. But even as early as Sunday morning when he sat through church with Grandma, he'd begun to suspect his feelings for Mattie were the real thing. She was delicate as a piece of china. He saw her melting brown eyes and shiny curls all during the hymn singing.

"Amazing Grace." That was her. The way she moved toward him, so shy but holding herself so straight. "How sweet the sound." That was her. Her quiet voice and silver laugh.

And it was kind of like magic how everything reminded him of her all week. People were all the time saying things that tied into his discovery of Mattie and Edward. Crystal's parents were going on a train trip, if you can believe it, and the first thing anybody said to him on Monday when he walked into the school yard was, "Did you ever ride a train?" Maybe that was just coincidence after all that time playing train with Edward, but it sure made the hair on the back of Jerry's neck bristle straight up.

Then, guess what one of the people in the book they were reading in class turned out to be named? *Martha,* that's all. And somebody else started talking about a haunted house, and all week long it went like that, just one thing after the other.

It was partly because of those coincidences that Jerry decided somebody was giving him a message. If he'd been Grandma, he'd have said for sure it was God. Or maybe it was fate. But definitely, he'd have had to be very dense not to see that clearly he was destined to fall in love with Mattie and spend his life giving her what protection he could. It would be a tragic life, but a noble one. He'd never have an ordinary wife like Crystal. He could never go bowling or out to eat pizza with Mattie. They wouldn't have an ordinary sex life like Mom and her boyfriend.

But what he could have with her could be so much rarer and finer than just regular marriages. Jerry sat and dreamed about all the things he could show Mattie, all the ways he could rig things to keep her safe and secret. Maybe, as time went on and she got less shy, he could introduce just a few of his friends to his secret family. He imagined how dumbfounded Clayton, grown-up and with a usual kind of wife and kids, would be.

"Might have known," he could hear Clayton exclaiming in amazement. "Might have known there was a mystery here since it was you, Jerry. But never, anytime, anyway, would I have thought of anything like this. It's incredibly great of you to protect her this way. Most guys would be making millions off something like this, but not you."

"Well, you're obviously feeling better, sitting around with a smile on your face like that one." Grandma broke into his thoughts on Friday afternoon. "Let me show you your Saturday dinner in the freezer while I'm thinking about it. Don't want you wasting away like a ghost in my house."

Jerry shook his head in amazement. It had been one thing after the other all week just telling him he had to belong with Mattie. "Don't worry about it, Grandma," he said, feeling wise. "There are worse things than ghosts in this world."

XVII

When he went to the museum on Saturday afternoon, the woman in the shop by the door spoke to him. "You were in here last Saturday, too, weren't you, son?" she said kindly. "Nice to see a boy your age into history like that. Can't pry my grandson away from those video games."

"I love history," Jerry said. "Old-timey stuff is awfully interesting." But since she'd noticed him, he worried that the woman might be watching for when he left. He decided he'd have to find a new place to hide until the museum closed. Lucky for him that Mattie had been so proud of showing him all the secret details of the huge old house. Behind one of the upstairs dormers was a spidery cubbyhole with a lattice door that let a little light through. Mattie had laughed, telling him that she and Edward used to play bear, hiding in the cubbyhole for a winter den.

"I would tell him all about how the snow was piling up outside and how even the birds were freezing. I would make us honey sandwiches and bring in pillows and we would pretend to hole up for the winter. He would watch for hunters at the slats."

The little dormer closet was in the Indian room upstairs. The room was deserted when Jerry tiptoed in. He looked over his shoulder, checking two or three times that nobody was coming. He nearly jumped out of his skin at the life-size figure standing by the tepee. Then, careful not to make noise, he twisted the latch and squeaked open the door to the crawl space under the rafters. He hunched down and eased himself into the dusty closet. He stuck his fingers in the slats to the door and pulled it almost completely shut, careful not to activate the latch and lock himself in. Nobody would notice that it was a tad loose, but he couldn't leave it really open. *Screeek.* He pulled it gingerly. *Click.* The latch engaged.

In a panic, Jerry shoved against the door. It wouldn't give. He was on his knees in the dark, locked in with spiders and probably rats. The blood drained from his head. He was ice-cold and breathing hard. Dumb, dumb, dumb. He felt like pounding his head on the floor. Like slitting his throat. How could anybody be such an idiot?

He closed his eyes, trying to calm himself. The space was so dark, it hardly mattered whether his eyes were open or not. He breathed slowly, telling himself to relax. When he opened his eyes in a few seconds, he could see dimly in the light filtering through the slats in the door. He moved his arms back, groping into the area around him. His left arm hit something soft. He pulled back, startled. Then, carefully, he reached and grazed it with the tips of his fingers, then folded it in his fingers and smiled. A pillow.

Mattie's pillow, left behind all that long time ago from her games with Edward. Finding it there at first made a shiver run through him. But once he got over the mystery of it, the pillow was a comfort. He clutched it on his knees, leaning his head down into it. He had to press his fingers against his lip to hold back a sneeze at the dust that floated from it. Eventually he plumped it behind him and lay back, knees curled. He'd wait for Mattie and Edward, call out to them. They couldn't work the latch, but together they'd think of something. He blushed. He wasn't going to let Mattie know he'd been clumsy enough to lock himself in here. That was for sure.

XVIII

Misting through from the tower, Mattie and Edward were bewildered not to find Jerry. Edward was crushed, so disappointed he gathered himself into a ball, his lip stuck out. If he could have cried, tears would have drizzled down his cheeks.

"It's your fault, Mattie," he whined. "You didn't like Jerry. You were mean to Jerry."

"I was not." Mattie didn't know what she felt. Relief, for one thing. Jerry wasn't coming. She wouldn't have to be part of Uncle's terrible plot to make him part of his experiments.

She knew what Uncle wanted. He wanted a way to slide *himself* from one life to the other, easy as a snake shedding its skin. To bypass, for himself, the horror of dying.

And Jerry was going to be a kind of trial run—

just to see if the new plan would work. Never mind if Jerry might like his life the way it was. Never mind if he might not want to become a ghost at the age of eleven. Or even—and Mattie shivered—suppose Uncle's new experiment didn't work? Suppose Jerry's light-body shattered, flew apart, when Uncle coaxed it out?

Uncle hoped that if he came out in some other way from his old body, he'd perhaps still be able to touch and feel. She and Edward kept some of their senses, after all. And they could speak. Perhaps if they had not had pain, they might still be able to feel. Perhaps if they had not been drained of strength, the new bodies would have been able to touch and move objects still. That was the sort of thing he was thinking, watching the two of them slantwise, sniffing at his bubbling beakers and poring over his dusty books. Over the years Mattie had almost learned to read his mind.

Now she stood in the hall beside the whimpering Edward and tried to tell herself how lucky it was that Jerry had not come back. How glad she was to be free of the awful burden of luring him into Uncle's trap.

But why, then, was there an ache at the back of her throat? Mattie looked at the puddles of moonlight on the carpet, beaming down from the high window over the door. She felt the darkness of all the years of loneliness washing over her. The misery of the pathetic life she was stranded in. She kept standing, but she wanted to crumple beside Edward and sob and sob. Why wasn't he here? Jerry, where are you? In that minute, she loved Jerry more than even Mama and Papa.

Thump. Thud. "Maaattie." A faint whisper of a sound, muffled, drifting down the stairs. She looked at Edward. His eyes widened. They went up the stairs, into Mama's old room where the museum had put the tepee and other Indian things. The noise was coming from the cubbyhole, where they'd played bear.

"Are you in there, Jerry?" Mattie went closer.

"Mattie! Yeah! It's me! Just after I got settled in here, the museum guy comes along and shoves the door shut." Their faint glow came through the slats and let him see the cobwebby rafters just over his head as he knelt beside the door. He'd thought there'd never be an end to being locked up in the dusty cave. During the hours of hunching there, straining to listen—first for the sound of people going, then for any sign that Mattie and Edward had returned, Jerry had nearly given up.

"Let him out, Mattie," Edward said expectantly. "Jerry got trapped."

"*How*, Edward? Let me think." Mattie was trembling with relief and distress. Jerry *was* a friend. He *had* come. She *wasn't* alone. And she couldn't let something awful happen to him. She'd tell him. About Uncle. Make him leave. Never come back. No matter what happened to her and to Edward. That's what she had to do.

"*I* know. Let's get Uncle. He won't mind. He can let Jerry loose." Edward's words floated in the chilly room like the dust motes that shone in the moonlight. Mattie stood still as stone.

"Your *uncle* is here?" Jerry sounded astonished. "Why didn't you say so before?"

XIX

"Hush, Edward." Mattie glared at her brother.
"Yes, Jerry. He is in the tower. I was going to tell
you. But we have to get you out first. We can't use
Uncle to get you out."

"Uncle *likes* Jerry. He wants us to have a friend.
You said I couldn't tell Jerry. Well I did. So there,
Mattie."

Mattie reached out with both hands. Edward
stared at her and jumped back just in time to stop
both of them from shattering into a rain of sparks.
"Uncle doesn't like anybody, Edward, you twit,"
she screamed. "Uncle is a monster." Mattie couldn't
imagine that she'd blurted all that out to Edward.
She stood stock-still with her hand over her mouth.

Edward's mouth sagged open.

"Oh, Edward," Mattie sobbed, touching his hair.
Edward looked toward the door, fearful.

Inside the cubbyhole, Jerry had turned to ice. What was Mattie saying? That she'd let him come here to be trapped by Ezekiel Gilchrist? He felt like a fool. All the time he'd been feeling sorry for her. Drooling over how beautiful she was. She was ugly. She was a demon. And if he didn't get out of here, he'd be dead. Fear made him twice as strong as usual. He hunched his shoulders and fell against the door. He balled his fists and pounded the edge by the latch. With a splintering noise, it finally broke free, and he crawled out onto the polished maple floor.

Mattie stepped back, out of his way, her curls swaying, almost covering her face. "You must leave, Jerry," she said. "You should not have come here— we should not have lured you. . . . I shouldn't have . . . " Her voice broke.

"Then how come you wrote me that note? How come you . . ." Jerry stopped. She *didn't* write him the note. How dumb that he hadn't seen. She couldn't pick up a pen, even hold a piece of paper. He ought to have known there was somebody else. If he'd had a grain of sense.

Mattie made a strangled noise. Then she went on. "I never meant . . . I was going to tell you. He said we had to, and before I knew you, I didn't care. I hated everybody outside for living the way we used to. Then, when you came and Edward started asking questions and everything started turning upside down I didn't know what to do. I knew Uncle might hurt you. His wheel—the magnetotron—he might use it to make you like us. I was not going to let you stay, Jerry. I was not. Believe me."

Jerry looked at her distraught face in the moonlight and did believe her. Afraid as he was, all the gentle feelings he had for her flooded back over him. "Let's *all* go," he said. "Let's leave now. You can stay in Grandma's basement while we figure out what to do. Nobody ever goes there but the meter man. There're plenty of boxes to hide behind."

"Can we? Let's go, Mattie. Let's run." Edward was too upset to stay. After what Mattie had said, there'd never be a way again to coax him into acting natural around Uncle.

"Are you sure?" She finally found the courage to look at Jerry. He smiled, but it was a twisted smile. He was terrified of Ezekiel Gilchrist.

"It's okay," he told her. "I can see what happened. You didn't see what else to do." Jerry's ears hummed. He could hardly swallow. "But let's go now. As fast as possible. Before Gilchrist shows up."

The basement of the house was the old kitchen. Mattie guided them down that way, to the back door that used to lead out to the garden. Jerry unfastened the chain and undid the bolt. They slid out the door and into the chilly fall night. Without saying a word, they paced single file to the iron fence at the back. The gate there was never locked. This time, Mattie and Edward faded through. Jerry unlatched it and followed them.

"You're going to have to hide somewhere nearby until it's really late," he said. There was a tall fir tree in the lot next to the museum. Mattie and Edward faded into the thickest part of it, beside the trunk. Jerry stayed out on the sidewalk.

Mattie shuddered. Outside she had nowhere to hide. Nothing was familiar. The tree wasn't enough protection. People could see them. She looked over her shoulder at the museum, the tower just visible from where they were. On the wind came the metal screech of the bird spinning, a sound like Uncle's rusty hinge voice—"Cheeldrin . . ." She had to be farther away to be safe. And not out in the open. She had to hide Edward inside somewhere.

Edward trembled like a field mouse. He clung to Mattie's hand and never said a thing. She knew he was terrified of the big world outside their fence. Terrified and enthralled. A motorized carriage whizzed past at a dizzying speed. Then another and another. They'd never been so close to one before. Never heard the humming of their engines. The carriages had white lights like bug eyes on the front that swept ahead of them. Mattie pulled Edward farther into the dark of the tree.

Jerry spotted a lawyer's office across the street, closed for the night. He pointed out the dark building. "You could go there. Late, when the traffic has died out, I'll come back for you."

"All right," Mattie said helplessly. She was quivering like a sea creature ripped from its shell.

Jerry watched for an empty space in the traffic. When everything was stopped at the light a block away, he gave Mattie and Edward the all clear. The two zipped across, a greenish blur that was absorbed in an instant by the brick wall of the lawyer's office on the other side. Jerry rubbed his eyes. He had no idea they could move that fast. As the cars approached after the light turned, the first driver in line rolled down his window.

"What was that weird light, kid?" a young guy in a Camaro called out to him.

Jerry looked mystified. "What light?" The truck behind the Camaro honked. The guy gave Jerry a funny look, rolled up his window, and drove on.

At home, Jerry felt embarrassed when he checked out Grandma's basement. Compared to what they were used to, it was shabby. He was bringing the girl he loved and wanted to protect to a grubby cement cave. Where was the little cottage in his

100

dreams, with the pretty porch and rosebushes? Where he'd pictured showing Mattie to Clayton? A parlor with soft-colored covers on the chairs. The basement was lit by a bare light bulb over Grandpa's old workbench. A lot of boxes were heaped on the floor. The place was a mess.

He'd make it all up to her someday. Hiding them in a place like this was only temporary, after all, until he could figure how to find them something suitable. But what could suit Mattie but a palace? Look at the house she'd lived in all her life. Even Grandma's house was pinched and tiny compared to that, forget the basement. Jerry had to remind himself, after all, he was saving them. "The Dr. Frankenstein of his day," the museum guy had said. Little did he know.

The way he felt about Mattie made all Jerry's dreams of being a hero—those times he'd thought about rushing into burning buildings, about collaring criminals—seem even more important. Now he had the chance to be a hero for real. Ezekiel Gilchrist was a danger to Mattie and Edward and him and everybody else as long as he was shut up in that tower with all his equipment. Jerry should drive him out into the open, cut him off from that wheel Mattie said was so important to his evil experiments.

Even at Grandma's, with familiar walls around

him, though, Jerry didn't feel quite the same as he used to in the old days, daydreaming about being brave. Thinking of going up against Ezekiel Gilchrist, to tell the truth, he didn't feel strong and important the way he had in those imagined scenes. The thought of taking on a person like that made him the slightest bit sick, to be honest. Jerry just hoped he wouldn't be a disgrace to Mattie, sticking her in a crummy basement and turning to jelly at the thought of having to protect her.

XX

Monday afternoon was the first chance Jerry had
to let Mattie and Edward up into Grandma's living
room. Sunday he'd crept out at one in the morning
to bring them from the lawyer's office. At Grandma's they'd gone in through her locked basement
door while he let himself quietly into the kitchen.
Sunday was so busy with church and Grandma's
fixing her special meat loaf for dinner that all Jerry
could manage was to sneak down once and ask if
they were okay. He was shy about facing them in
the grubby hiding place he'd found for them, but
they seemed too grateful to notice the mess.

"Sorry to leave you by yourselves so long," he
told them after school on Monday, when he finally
had some time free. "Would you like to come upstairs and take it easy awhile?" Grandma had a

funeral to clean after and wouldn't be back before six. He felt kind of unsure how to entertain them now that they were here.

"Thank you very much. You're sure we won't be in the way?" Mattie was shy, self-conscious because she had gone along with Uncle's plot at first. What must Jerry really think of her?

"Let's go!" Edward was his usual self. He charged for the stairs, Mattie behind.

They looked around Grandma's house the way Jerry had at theirs—as if *they* were in a museum. "What's this?" Edward kept wanting to know. He pointed at Grandma's stereo and then at the TV.

"Edward!" Mattie said in a stern voice. "You know it's rude to point." She stared, too, at the gray glass square.

"That's what I told you about, Mattie," Jerry said. "You know, the television. It has pictures. And sound." He picked up the remote and turned it on. Mattie jumped as the music blared and the picture came on screen. A man was singing, rocking backward with a mike in his hand, and the image of a girl in tights was superimposed, dancing. Then the screen split in four and there were cats' faces, with fangs bared, then it was back to one image of a man walking out of a jail cell with a beard down to his chest. Then a subway train that was scrawled all over whizzed past and all of a sudden there was a green field with daisies.

Mattie's eyes were huge. Edward had his nose practically against the screen. "How did they get in?" he asked Jerry. "Can *we* go inside?"

"It's pictures, Edward," Mattie said, feeling almost as bewildered as he was but proud she knew that much. "Isn't it, Jerry? Pictures that move and speak."

"Like us?" Edward was not convinced he couldn't get inside. "With new bodies?"

"No," Jerry told him. "It's different. Those are just pictures, like Mattie says. They can't really talk. It's just a record—just that somebody caught what they looked like and said and all with a machine that shows it back."

"Similar to a stereopticon, Edward," Mattie said. "Only fancier." Papa had bought one of those and they'd all looked at pictures of castles in Europe through the viewing tube.

"*Very* fancier," Edward said. He didn't think it was really the same thing at all. Edward thought Jerry's grandma's television was the most amazing thing he'd ever seen. He balled up his fists, bent his knees, and began to sway and jump to the music.

The sound was confusing to Mattie, jumbled and loud, not like music. And the pictures changed so fast she was dizzy watching. What was that? Was it a red fox? It had a furry tail, but it was gone and now there was a pair of bright red lips mouthing words all by themselves and then a man juggling two goldfish bowls—how could he do that?—and then a woman wearing so little Mattie glowed with embarrassment and then a big rainstorm with umbrellas blowing inside out and then . . . She looked away, bewildered.

"You might like a regular program better than MTV," Jerry said. He clicked around the dial. Somebody was potting plants on the educational station. He stopped for a minute. The guy was chunking a big red geranium into a white pot.

"With winter coming on, we could all use a touch of color," the man was saying. "No need to fade into the woodwork like ghosts just because the day is gray. Keep a splash of color around." Jerry winced and clicked again. This time he came up on a soap opera with a couple pulling off each other's clothes. He rapidly clicked back to MTV.

"Let Edward dance," he said. "You'll get used to it after a while." But Mattie sat on Grandma's soft sofa, so different from Mama's horsehair one, trying not to be obvious looking around the tiny house where Jerry lived. Cozy. She told herself it was cozy. But she yearned for the shadows and mystery of Mama's floor-to-ceiling red velvet drapery. The

106

curving stairs, twisting past where she could see. In Grandma's living room, Mattie felt she'd be stared at.

The way the TV jumped from one thing to another confused Mattie and made her feel they had been wrong to leave home. This outside world was all changed. These new people wanted something different every second. Jerry told her his grandma had just bought new furniture, "a living room set." He seemed very proud. "She's planning to buy a big screen TV that'll take up that whole corner once she pays off the sofa and all," he explained.

Mattie had a dizzy feeling that she would just become accustomed to something out here only to have it snatched away and replaced by something different. Mama had had new covers made, but their dark carved furniture was always the same. It had belonged to Papa's mother in Germany. Mattie tried not to look around at the room in a way that Jerry would notice, but it seemed to her full of temporary things. Vases and pictures that would be thrown out and replaced by new ones. It was all part of the TV world where magically everything turned new every few minutes. Mattie hated to admit it and hoped she would understand better later, but this new world looked too frantic to her. She did not feel safe here.

"You and Edward will be all right here," Jerry

said. "But what about your uncle? Can't we just forget about him now?" His voice shook a little. He was hoping Mattie would pretend, the way he felt like doing, that they did not have to think about Ezekiel Gilchrist shut up in his tower.

Mattie shuddered. "He will keep on with his plan. You escaped from him and Edward and I are gone, but he'll find a way to lure someone to his tower. I can't let that happen. I ought to go back, take Edward, now that you are safe. . . . There must be something . . . " But her voice broke. Disturbed as she was by the world outside, Mattie had no illusions about Uncle's wrath if she returned. She had no idea what he might do. The thought made her tremble.

"No," Jerry said, making his voice as firm as possible. "I'm in this with you. Don't forget that. We could go to the police. Tell the museum people."

"Oh, *no*." Mattie caught his eye. "We should be exposed then, all three of us. Edward would be a sideshow freak. Mama would never forgive me." She stifled a sob and buried her hands in her curls. Mama had felt it was unladylike for a young woman to have her name in the paper. Imagine how she'd feel with Mattie and Edward stared at by a whole country on television sets. Electrical oddities . . . *ghosts*? Mattie cringed back into the sofa cushions.

She would rather take her chances with Uncle than be humiliated that way.

So far, she was Mattie still. In the outside world, become a freak, she might as well change her name. Out here, even now, she had trouble holding to her familiar thoughts of Mama and Papa, the memories of how it had been. Time made the world different. She was the only unchanging thing, a cork bobbing in the vastness. At home the old walls had guarded her, told her she was who she had always been.

"We have to find a way to stop his wheel, his magnetotron," Mattie said, pulling herself up straight. "Uncle could harm no one without that. And he could not rebuild it without seeking outside the tower for supplies. Outside, who knows? He might mend his ways. He might work to make your television even more wonderful. Perhaps he would think of a new project. Anyway, it would take him years to rebuild the magnetotron the way he has it now. He told me how many windings of wire he needed, how carefully the copper had to be polished for months on end."

Jerry felt a little encouraged. "Could we sneak in through the tunnel and destroy it while he sleeps? Is he a real sound sleeper?"

Mattie shook her head and sighed. "He doesn't sleep; he goes into a kind of trance sitting beside the singing wheel, but he hears every bat stir. The highest, faintest cheep that they make he knows about. I've seen it on his face. No, you could never surprise him that way."

They sat side by side, depressed. Then, Mattie's face lit up.

"There is a way. A perfect way. We will not have to disturb Uncle at all."

"Tell me." Jerry tried his best not to feel there had to be a catch.

"The tower," Mattie said, her face glowing, "and the iron bird. Uncle only just explained to Edward and me that the bird keeps his magnetotron from overheating. If it overheats, it melts. It's so simple. All we need to do is to cut the wire to the bird."

"And how could we do that?" Jerry had a sinking feeling he knew, but he hoped he was wrong.

Mattie looked at him, surprised. He was not as excited as she had expected. "Well, of course, *you* would actually do it, but Edward and I would help."

"Do what?" Jerry asked.

"Climb the tower, of course," Mattie exclaimed. "Cut the wire where it makes the bird turn."

XXI

"There's a ladder," Jerry said in a tight voice. "I saw it when we were looking at the tower from the bus, on the school trip. Kind of rusty and broken, I guess."

"Yes," Mattie said. "Of course, there is! Uncle used to climb up there to adjust the wires before Mama and Papa died, before he went into the tower for good." To Mattie, that time was yesterday. She didn't stop to think how snaggletoothed and rickety a ladder would become in more than a hundred years of disuse. And she and Edward floated as high as they liked. For her, the fear of falling was so far in the past she barely recalled it.

Jerry crimped and uncrimped his fingers, trying to warm up his suddenly cold hands. "You're sure cutting the wire to the bird would turn off his machine?" He was just stalling. The minute she'd said it, he'd understood. The bird had been spinning mysteriously way up there with no wind for miles. They'd talked about it on the bus. It was true, all right. All they needed was somebody with guts enough to climb the tower and unfasten the connection. And wasn't he, Jerry, the guy dying to be a hero anytime he had the chance? Just waiting for a building to catch on fire or a kid to fall through some ice?

"Oh, yes, Uncle was quite clear," Mattie said. "He was bragging about how no one had thought to wonder at the bird's spinning."

"I wonder how high that tower *is*?" Jerry mused, as if he thought it was just an interesting question to speculate about.

"I remember Papa saying it was seventy-five feet tall," Mattie said. "He was talking to Uncle about his climbing it all the time. . . . " Her voice died down. Papa had been cautioning Uncle on the danger. She had forgotten that side of it. "That is high for you to go, Jerry," she said, beginning to guess what he was thinking. "I'd forgotten."

"Oh, don't worry," Jerry said. "Don't give it a second thought. I wasn't. Seriously. I was just curious, that's all. If I'm going to climb something, I like to know what I'm up against. That's all. It'll be a cinch. Piece of cake."

Well, it wasn't the Sears Tower, after all. Just a

teeny tower five stories high or so. With a ladder. And vines grew up most of it. It just wasn't the sort of thing Jerry had ever thought of when he day-dreamed about ways of showing how brave he was. And there was so long to think it over. With the crooks robbing people and fires and all, you'd just walk up on them and before you knew it, the whole thing was over. Now, he'd have to plan, look for rubber-handled wire cutters and screwdrivers among his grandpa's old tools in the basement. Walk around with this lump of ice in his stomach and his knees weak until they had the chance to get started.

"Let's go tonight," he said. "The longer we leave him there, the more chance he might hurt some-body." If Jerry had to act normal around Grandma and try to eat and do the usual things for more than a few hours, she'd know something was up, the way he was feeling now.

"Jerry, that is very brave," Mattie told him, lean-ing toward him, her eyes warm. "Not many people in this world would just decide to do such a brave thing without giving it a second thought."

The ice in his belly melted a little. He felt taller and thinner. "It's just what anybody would do, Mattie," he said. "We can't leave a menace like that out there to hurt innocent people."

"Edward and I will climb with you," Mattie said.

"Of course, for us, that part of it will be different."
She was trying to be delicate about how he might
break his neck but they couldn't. For them, it would
be fun, Jerry realized, jealous. Just floating up in the
air like birds, no fear of falling. "I wish we could
help you cut the wire, carry something, *do* more."

When Jerry heard the note of sadness in her voice,
he stopped feeling envious. Mattie was miserable to
be leaving it all to him, miserable to be stuck in this
unnatural shadow of a body her uncle had left her.

The sharp smell of spruce stung Jerry's nose as
the three of them crowded at the base of the tower.
It was just after midnight. Jerry's courage nearly
failed when he reached for the first rung in the snaggletoothed ladder. It was sharp with rust and almost
cut through the wool gloves he'd been smart enough
to wear.

The rung he'd grabbed was chest height. He
pulled himself up and fitted his right foot onto the
first rung and started to climb. Just one at a time,
he told himself, one at a time. He needn't think how
high he was going. Each step was just a little farther
than the one before. Mattie floated a little ahead of
him, with Edward beside her. The enormous spruce
hid them all for the first two stories. Overhead the
bird twirled, shrieking its ugly chant of metal against
metal.

"We are safe," Mattie exulted. "As long as the bird turns, we know he is on the wheel."

Jerry, sweating, pulled himself up another step—the ladder swayed with his weight as he pulled even with the second floor. Some of the bolts had pulled loose. Jerry felt his stomach float free and swallowed hard. His foot slipped in a tangle of vines that massed above the second story. He grabbed the edges of the ladder with both hands and hung on, ice-cold. He was sweating, but he couldn't turn loose to wipe his eyes. His hands were frozen to the ladder. For a second he thought he couldn't go on.

"Jerry's slow." Edward's voice floated down to him from the roof. They were waiting where the tower passed the roof of the house proper, beside a dormer.

"Hush, Edward. Jerry is doing the very best he can." Mattie tried to keep the impatience from her own voice. Jerry kept sliding and thrashing in the vines and at times she thought he was caught. Uncle had gone hand over hand up the ladder, steady, if slow. She pushed away the thought that if she had only had a normal body, she could have climbed faster.

What did they think he was? The bolts beside his hand screeched in pain and the ladder shuddered when Jerry put his weight back on the rung. He swallowed, squeezed his sweaty hands inside the gloves, and climbed on. The bulky tools he'd stuffed into his jacket pockets poked his ribs. One rung, then the next. When a rung was too loose, Jerry held on to the sides for dear life and pulled himself to the next. The tree was below him now but he didn't dare look down. The sound of the bird was louder, an almost unbearable screech as he cleared the roof of the house.

Another twenty feet and he was at the edge of the tower roof, where there was a ledge. Three feet wide—enough, if Jerry didn't look down. Unfortunately, he did, and swayed. His stomach heaved at the awful drop. Just a little he started to wet his pants. The ladder was bolted to the curve of the tower roof. Jerry dropped to his knees and caught hold of it. Stars were spread out above him. He felt for a second that he was in the sky, clutching the rusty iron ladder and hurtling through space. He closed his eyes and the dizziness passed.

Mattie and Edward were beside the bird, waiting as he pulled himself the last distance up. He ducked, climbing onto the narrow walkway as the bird swung just over his head, one wing grazing his hair. "Come on," Edward urged.

"It's pretty up here," Mattie called to him over the shrieking of the metal bird. "Look at the lake sparkling off yonder."

"No, thanks." Jerry tried not to look at anything but the iron rod that supported the bird. As he'd hoped, the wires were bolted on just above the edge of the roof. Jerry's jacket was bulging with the cutters, a screwdriver, and, stuck into his belt, a hammer, in case the wires were corroded on. Grandpa had left all the tools he needed.

"Stand back," he said. "I see what to do." It was clear he had to pull the wires loose. The insulation still looked good, if frayed, but he'd only hold to rubber when he touched it. Jerry knelt on the narrow ledge at the very top of the tower, clutching for balance at the last rung of the ladder, and gingerly reached for the first wire with the skinny pincers of Grandpa's old wire cutters. He pulled and yanked and for a minute thought he'd never free the wire from the bolt. On the third try, in a shower of sparks, he cut the wire loose. Jerry bent backward, gasping, to avoid the glowing end that hissed like a snake as he ripped it from under the bird.

The terrible screeching began to soften. The spinning slowed, slowed. Stopped. Silence. The sudden quiet made them all stare in wonder. A car swished past, miles below. A dog barked off in the distance somewhere.

"You did it, Jerry." Mattie's voice was a whisper. "You knew just what to do." A sharp smell began to rise from the wire that Jerry had pulled loose. Hot metal and burning insulation. A faint curl of smoke wisped in the air past Jerry's nose.

Jerry began inching himself backward, feeling for the rungs of the ladder with his feet and hands. He slid back onto the ladder, inching himself down the tower wall to the ground.

XXII

Never in a thousand years did Jerry think he'd sleep. As soon as he shut his eyes, all he saw was the stone of the tower, moving past his face as he climbed. He felt the cold oozing from the granite against his cheek as he inched his way up. Just on the edge of sleep, he'd feel the ladder sway, dipping under him, leaving him clutching the vines that tangled along beside. After he'd started violently under the sheets, kicking in a way that scared Grandma's cat—she'd come in to warm up under his comforter—Jerry did begin to relax.

He had done it, after all. The magnetotron was no longer a danger. Jerry had to feel a little proud, though not the way he'd expected to in those scenes he'd made up. Now mostly he was glad it was over; he hoped never to see another seventy-five-foot tower as long as he lived. He stretched out on the sheets and felt good that Mattie was safer. He'd kept her from confronting her uncle. That would have been brave, but it would have led nowhere.

"Listen to this, Jerry." Grandma called him in from the bathroom to listen to the radio in the morning. "Strange doings at the museum."

Jerry rushed into the kitchen. A reporter was just interviewing Mr. Johnson at the museum as he sank into his chair.

"Smoke damage was confined to the tower?" the man asked.

"Completely. A tunnel was exposed, giving access to the tower, which turns out to be an old laboratory, undoubtedly once belonging to Ezekiel Gilchrist. A boulder beside the carriage house, operated by a lever, turned out to be the doorway. It was left open; someone evidently was hiding inside and made his escape when the wiring short-circuited. We assume a homeless person stumbled on the entrance and was sleeping there. Perhaps he or she began playing with Ezekiel Gilchrist's old wiring and caused the smoke damage. We ought to be grateful. Otherwise, we'd never have uncovered the fascinating space inside the tower."

"You'll be adding the laboratory to the museum exhibits?"

120

"You can bet on it. It's a major find, no question about that."

So Gilchrist was gone. Mattie thought he'd hitch a ride on a freight and go on to Milwaukee or even Chicago. Gilchrist had always felt that East Bent was too small for him. He'd never come back, Jerry felt sure of that. Not with half the town snooping through his laboratory.

"Grandma, I was using some tools. I want to take them back before I forget." Jerry put the cereal box down without pouring any. He was halfway down the basement steps before she could tell him to at least have some cereal before he dashed off. Grandma shook her head.

Mattie was sitting a foot off the floor, her feet tucked in under her skirt, lost in thought. When Jerry came around behind the packing boxes and saw her, he almost hesitated to speak and shatter her mood.

"Mattie," he said gently, "you were right. Your uncle's gone. He left the tunnel open, and now they'll make the tower part of the museum."

A shadow passed over her face. The room where she'd sat for so many years with Edward wouldn't be private anymore. Uncle and his humming wires would no longer be up the spiral stairs. Change at last had come to their closed-in world. She shuddered a little. Still, Mattie knew that was the way it had to be.

"You were wonderful to do what you did, Jerry," she said. "Uncle could not stay there. He might have killed somebody. Now perhaps he will find a way to add to the wonders of your world. Make your television even more a marvel."

"What he was doing was pretty amazing—getting you and Edward to live on the way you have, aiming toward living forever himself. That's as incredible as anything anybody has done."

Mattie nodded, clearly not wanting to discuss Uncle's attempts at immortality any further. "Soul and Spirit are Fraud! The Electric is Life!" That had been his chant. But it was not true, Mattie thought. Now that Uncle was gone, she was free. Free to think her own thoughts. Before she had told herself over and over that he was a genius. And he was. But geniuses were not always right. Electricity was not everything. Spirit was not a fraud. Nor was Soul. Mattie knew in her heart that was true.

She and Edward were shaped of Uncle's electrical force, but that was not *all* they were. What about Edward? For all these years and years, she'd cared for him. Was that electricity? No, it was love. And look at Jerry. He had climbed the tower last night, risking his life to help them and to save innocent people from Uncle. That was spirit, no matter what Uncle said.

When Mama and Papa had been killed, Mattie had strained to hear if there were voices on the wind, any words coming to her from the place where they had gone. She had stood in their big bedroom that summer, with the windows open and the white curtains billowing with the breeze, and listened and listened. The wind was like the ocean, she felt. It swept other shores, perhaps the mysterious place of those who had gone on. They were somewhere. They had been here and now they were somewhere.

Jerry went back upstairs, not wanting Grandma to come looking for him. Mattie was left with her thoughts. Edward was at the other end of the basement watching out the high window to see the passing feet of children on their way to school. They could go home now. The tower would not be a shelter for them any longer, but Mattie knew crannies in the attic, dim nooks in the basement that would serve to hide them days while the museum buzzed around them. Jerry would be disappointed. Mattie smiled, but she sighed, too, at the dreams she'd had of Jerry as her suitor.

Out in the world, she'd quickly seen how futile those dreams were. They were sweet, especially since she knew Jerry shared them. She had had a lover, after all. Those plans twirling in the leaves weren't all for naught. But their worlds were different. Mattie could never adapt to the fast changes all around her outside. She did not want to. She wanted the dear old things, the dear old life, Mama and Papa and her own friends, not to hide—a freak—in a world that had gone on and on past all her memories and filled itself with strangeness and change.

They'd go back to the old house, she and Edward. With Uncle gone, that thought had a new appeal. Without him there, she knew the Before Time would come closer. Already she was beginning to feel presences she'd never felt, focused so closely on Uncle and his demands. There, in Jerry's basement, she could almost feel Mama's arm reaching to comfort her, hear Papa's teasing chuckle. Cook and Michael the gardener leaning on his rake and her friends from school. She was remembering them all. Only it was almost more than memory. Presences. Even once, Amanda Buckley, the last person she would have wanted to see, prissing and preening in India muslin embroidered in pink and yellow butterflies. Nose in the air as always, she flounced toward Mattie in the dimness of Jerry's basement, then faded into sparkling dust motes.

"Edward," she said slowly, almost dreading explaining to him that they had to return to the old ways. He'd been so excited by all the wonders of the outside world. He came toward her, a thoughtful look on his face. He spoke before she could.

"Let's go back, Mattie," he said. "Home. I want to go home." Mattie stared, astonished.

"But I thought you were happy here, Edward. I thought you loved Jerry's house."

"It's not good for train," he said evasively. She could see something else was bothering him.

"Is that all, Edward? Why else do you want to go back?"

"Mama told me. She said. Come home."

Mattie was shaken. Edward never talked about Mama and Papa and the Before Time. He liked those memories filtered through her. She sensed they were too strong for him otherwise. "When did Mama tell you, Edward?"

"Just now. While I was at the window." He was feeling her presence, too, then, now that Uncle was no longer ruling their lives. It was as if Uncle had blocked out those other, gentler beings from making contact. Or perhaps it was she and Edward—they had always thought about what Uncle was doing, what Uncle wanted.

That afternoon, explaining to Jerry was not as painful as Mattie had feared. She was concerned he would think they didn't like his house, that they thought his new world was ugly.

"Your world is wonderful, Jerry," she told him. "But it is too different for us. Too fast and full of change. We need to go back and try to find the place where we belong."

"But surely, hiding off in an attic all day..." Jerry hesitated. What else were they doing at his place, after all? "All this is temporary. When I'm older I can get you a place of your own where no one will ask questions. A little apartment or a house, even, where you can live secretly. Maybe gradually get to know just a few people, nice ones you could trust." He knew while he was saying it, he was being foolish. How long before he'd be in a position to set them up in an apartment, much less a house? How many years of skulking behind packing boxes would that amount to?

"You're talking about giving up your life for us," Mattie said. "I can't tell you how much it means that you've been willing to do that." As she told him that, Mattie knew how deeply she meant what she said. What Jerry had done, what he offered was more than the dreams she'd had of suitors bringing roses, of dance cards filled and heads turning when she swept into a ball. What Jerry offered was sweeter and simpler than that. But it would never work.

126

Their worlds were too different. *She* was too different. For a short time, he'd given her the feeling she was a girl, just a normal girl again. That was a dream, but it was a dream she had ached to experience and now, thanks to Jerry, she had.

"That's all right," Jerry said, wishing he could think of something more flowery to say. "I was glad to do it."

"We'll go back tonight," Mattie said, "when it's too late for motor carriages on the streets. You needn't come with us; now we know the way."

"I'll come see you again, like before," Jerry said eagerly. "Maybe we could meet under the spruce tree by the tower so I wouldn't have to hide inside again. I think they're watching now because of doors being left unlocked those other times."

"My cave," Edward said, remembering the Before Time.

Mattie was quiet for a long time. Jerry thought at first she wasn't going to answer. His feelings were beginning to be hurt. Maybe she was sick of him, looking for a way to tell him to get lost.

"We'll always want to be with you, Jerry, as long as we are in this world, won't we, Edward?" Edward nodded solemnly, seeming to feel it was a serious kind of pledge he was called upon to make. Jerry was a little puzzled. All they were doing, after all, was arranging to meet. But he had a funny feeling at the pit of his stomach that something else was up. Something they were aware of that he wasn't.

Anyway, that's the way they left it. Mattie and Edward left the basement in the middle of the night and returned to their own house. Jerry counted the days until Saturday when Grandma had another wedding to deal with and he could wait for them under the spruce.

He got there around seven when it was good and dark. The moon wasn't up and the branches were thick enough to block the faint shine from their bodies, he was sure. He didn't know what direction to watch. They might float from up above or rise from the cellar, who knew? Anyway, he settled against the wall of the museum and waited. He'd brought Mattie a plastic rose from Grandma's vase—a white one. Grandma wouldn't miss it. He sat and waited and waited, the cold beginning to seep through his jeans and jacket. He checked his watch. Seven-thirty. It wasn't like Mattie to be late.

There was something he wasn't facing. Jerry knew that, but he was determined not to unless he had to. Mattie's hints. She'd kind of almost suggested that they might not be coming. She was too delicate to tell him straight out, but Jerry had sensed it in the distant look she'd gotten in her eyes, the kind of happy shine that came over her face when she spoke of her mama and papa and the friends she'd had before. It was almost like she was planning to see them soon. He'd had the feeling that she and Edward might have decided to leave the half bodies Ezekiel Gilchrist had left them and go on. But Mattie hadn't wanted to tell him right out.

He sat against the wall and shivered and more and more had to admit to himself that they were gone. He felt miserable, betrayed. He understood Mattie's not telling him if that's what she'd decided. Maybe it wasn't an easy decision. Maybe until the last minute she'd wavered back and forth. She hadn't wanted to be a freak, caught in a world she didn't fit into. All his talking hadn't made her feel different. And in a way, he could see it. *Would* he have been able to have her forever for a spirit-wife? What about when he was fifty and she was still twelve? What about having babies and going bowling and shooting pool and all? Could he honestly say that his whole life he'd give up all that to protect Mattie, beautiful as she was, much as he loved her?

Being honest was sad. Tears came to Jerry's eyes, though, of course, they could have been partly from the cold. His nose ran a little and he stood up to fish for a Kleenex in his pocket. Wouldn't you think, though, he thought bitterly, that if they had decided to give up, to move on to wherever their mama and papa had gone, wouldn't you think they'd at least figure a way to leave him a message? Sure, it was hard, since they couldn't hold a pen and all, but wouldn't you think they'd figure something and not leave him sitting in the cold waiting for nothing?

The moon finally came up and a beam or two stole through the thick spruce branches, lighting up spots on the tree like a search beam. That's how Jerry finally did see the message Mattie had struggled to leave behind for him on the trunk of the tree. It was a heart, scorched into the bark by the electric force from her finger. Inside, she'd written "J.R. and M.G." for all the world to see. So she did love him, Jerry thought, putting his own hand gently over the spot. She left, but she loved him.

He stood for a while feeling the place on the trunk, spelling the letters with his finger. Finally, he put the white rose he'd brought in the branch just above the heart.

He stayed there for another half hour, thinking over what had happened. Just as he was about to leave, stooping down low to crawl from under the limbs, he saw the place where Mattie had helped

Edward, too, bid him farewell. Scrawled in wobbly letters nearer the bottom of the trunk, he saw "CHOO." Edward's last train call, thanking him for playing his favorite game.

SARAH SARGENT studied English literature as an undergraduate at Randolph-Macon Woman's College. Later, she received her master's degree from Yale University, where she was a Woodrow Wilson fellow. Born and raised in Virginia, she now lives in Oshkosh, Wisconsin, and teaches at the University of Wisconsin–Oshkosh.

Like East Bent, Oshkosh has a museum in a mansion that was once a private home. "That influenced my thinking for this book," the author says. "As a child, going into museums that used to have people living in them intrigued me. I wondered whether there were 'presences' around."

Sarah Sargent is married and has two children. She is the author of several books for young people, including *Jonas McFee, A.T.P.* and *Seeds of Change* (both Bradbury Press).